A CHILD'S WOUND

The characters and events in this book are fictitious. Any similarity to real persons, alive or deceased, is coincidental and not intended by the author.

Copyright © 2009 by Dwayne Kavanagh

All rights reserved. The use of any part of the publication, reproduced, transmitted in any form or by any means electronic, mechanical, photocopying, recording, or otherwise, or stored in a retrieval system without the prior written consent of the publisher; or in the case of photocopying or other reprographic copying-- license from the Canadian Copyright Licensing agency— is an infringement of copyright law.

ISBN: 978-0-9813233-0-5

For Nicky

ONE

On the other side of the window people flowed down the cold wet sidewalk passing one another, and not one made eye contact with the other. A woman walked by the window as if she was held back by gale force winds. A scarf wrapped tightly around her face.

Inside, Tim found solace in his coffee as Dave Matthew's chocolate-coal voice poured out from the speaker above, drowning out the melodic Baristas that sung back orders to the cashiers. Coffee fanatics filled the room, snaking through the display of oversized coffee cups labeled with words of wisdom. Tim noticed a Cuisinart coffeemaker edging off of the display and he reached across the aisle and pushed it back out of harm's way.

He saw her slide through the line-up and her dress caught a button as she squeezed between two men, revealing her cleavage. Two pairs of eyes: one in awe, one in disgust. Oblivious to the event, she moved through the crowd with a red leather coat draped over her arm. A fiery aura manifested around her straight strawberry hair, reflecting from the light above. It contrasted with her dark hazel eyes. Looking up from his cup, he made eye contact and flashed an interested smile. The look caught her off guard and lingered long enough to become personal.

Rising from the table, he walked toward her as she approached. He folded a newspaper in his hand. Within a breath of her, he turned and sidled as she slipped past. Not saying a word. Glancing back, he noticed her milky white skin turn a light shade of pink. She looked back at him, frozen. Ready, smiling, his soft eyes engaged. Her color began to fade away: white again. Her head slowly moved from side to side and as if she was on a runway, she strutted toward the back of the line, waiting to place her order. In line, she checked her watch, and reapplied her lipstick.

Picking up the creamy latte, she moved toward a pair of leather bucket chairs in the back. She reclined into the comfort of the brown chair, laying her coat over the arm.

He slid the folded newspaper into a wooden rack on the floor beside the counter.

Shoulders back, hands swinging in rhythm at his sides, Tim approached with confidence.

"Hi. Do you mind if I sit down?"

She looked up and acknowledged the comment as if to say it's up to you but she didn't directly answer the question. They enjoyed a few seconds of silence as he took off his brown suede sports jacket. He observed her brush away the hair covering her face.

"Getting out of the rain?" he asked.

"My hair is a disaster."

"Really? I hadn't noticed."

She laughed off his subtle compliment and he watched a small pink cloud surface on the skin of her cheeks.

"Thank you. I think, I'm Simone," she said.

He sipped the remainder of his green tea latte and the sweet and sour flavor soaked his palate. He studied her every movement and some of the signs he knew to look for were there.

"My name's Tim," he said.

"Look I'm not here to get picked up if that's what you're thinking."

He savored the comment, touched it, and released it into the warm air. He grinned.

"Wasn't my intent. You're not my type."

She crossed her legs toward him. "Oh you're one of those guys."

"You're funny. No. Not quite."

She sipped her latte, all the while never losing eye contact. "So what's your type then?"

"I thought you weren't interested in getting picked up?"

"I'm not saying I am but tell me anyway."

He kept the conversation flowing as he described his ideal mate and she responded as if stung by each of the characteristics that were direct opposites of her.

"For example, look at what you're wearing today."

"Why? What's wrong with what I'm wearing?"

"It's pouring rain. It's cold. Here, look at that woman over there in line."

"Who, the lady dressed like a man in a suit?"

"You see she's prepared for the weather. Classy."

"So you think I have no class?" she asked.

"That's not what I said. I said I usually go for women that are a little more elegant and let's say a lot less flamboyant."

"Oh, so you like girls who wear pants is that it?"

He laughed at the comment but she seemed serious. He silenced the laugh and pretended to ponder her question.

"There's something about you that intrigues me," he said.

"Oh…like?"

"I can't pinpoint it yet. You're exotic but it's not only your looks."

The compliment struck a chord, positive vibes resonated from her hazel eyes, and this was a good sign.

"Go on," she said.

"Maybe I misjudged you. Maybe inside that beautiful shell is a woman with confidence—with intellect. A lady of the arts."

"I know I'm stylish...there's no doubt about that. But I'm relevant too. I may attend more fashion shows than Charity Events. Can't fault me there...it's just my thing. I am into art though."

"Is that so?"

"That's so. I hear there's a great Picasso exhibit at the MET. Have you seen it?" Simone asked as she leaned toward him.

"No I haven't," he lied.

"I haven't seen it yet either. I hear it's dark."

"You mean mysterious?" he asked.

She moved closer. Their knees touched. Her dress slid up revealing her salt-white thighs, "Yes that too, but I mean the rooms are dark or something. Anyway, that's what my sister said."

"So your sister's the aficionado?"

"Yeah, she's the expert. I just like looking at the paintings. She works at a gallery on Park Avenue. You should check it out."

Tim looked at his watch with an expression of concern. He made sure she had a full view of what he was doing. "Simone, my time is important to me and I never waste a moment of it, so let me extend you an offer."

"I'm listening."

"Let's grab another coffee and head over to the MET. You've made it clear that you're not looking to be picked up and that's fine. Consider us just two friends hanging out on a rainy day."

After a moment of silence, Simone's eyes met his. Searching. Open. "Friends huh?"

"Friends," he said while reaching for her hand. He helped her out of the chair and wrapped her coat around her slender shoulders. He took the time to brush her hand, stealing a caress of her skin.

He opened the door and the wind hit them with no remorse, attacking their faces with pellets of rain. He wrapped his arm around her shoulder and ushered her toward the subway entrance. Everyone around them had the same idea. The group ran for shelter, jamming down the staircase. Shoulders rubbing, their hips grinding, transferring evidence of their encounters.

On the platform, they waited for the number 5 train to 86 Street. They flirted, exchanging quick smiles and long glances. Huddled, they entwined their fingers. Their shouts sounded like whispers over the roar from the oncoming train as they exchanged small talk.

The two walked up the stairs to the sidewalk above. The sun tore through the grey clouds and the warmth washed over their faces.

"Crazy weather this time of year," Tim said.

Simone agreed.

They walked hand in hand for three blocks until the entrance to the MET rose medieval in front of them. Cement spikes lined the rim of the roof, topping the stone walls outside. They took the steps two at a time to reach the main entrance. Through the doors, they entered a great hall with sunrays beaming down from the windows above. Walls of stone echoed the view from outside, giving off the same medieval vibe. He paid the forty-dollar fee and handed Simone a guide to the exhibit.

"I never get enough of this place," she said.

"I know what you mean. Imagine us locked in here after dark?"

Simone flashed a wink and a smile. "Sounds exciting."

"Imagine the trouble you and I could get into."

"Is that a dare, Tim?"

Tim flashed back a wink of his own. "I knew you would be fun."

Exiting the second floor, two ominous stone statues guarded the moon gate entrance to the Chinese Garden Court.

"It's this way."

They continued along the hallway, passing the Japanese Buddhist Altar and the final turn brought them to the Picasso exhibit.

The long room twisted in front of them. A worn wooden chair in the corner angled out to the middle of the room and the original white paint had all but chipped away. Dimmed lighting washed the room in a sea of light grey. The effect darkened the room. Brushed pewter lighting hung from the walls above each painting and sprayed light on the canvases. Picasso's works, stood out as a bright beacon among the shadows.

"This is the Picasso self portrait," he said.

"Hmmmm...Handsome. I love the dark coat and the beard. Makes him look mysterious, but his eyes look sad."

Simone locked her arm with his as they moved along to the next painting. "La Vie 1903" almost filled the height of the wall and towered before them. Simone studied the painting. She folded her arms and placed the back of her hand underneath her chin. Tim thought she was trying too hard but he liked that.

"What do you think?"

"I'm wondering who the old woman is and why the two nude lovers look scared," she said.

"Some people believe that the nude man is Carlos Casagemas."

"Who's that?" she asked.

"Carlos was one of Picasso's closest friends."

"Oh."

"It gets better"

"Really?" Simone snuggled closer and whispered in his ear. "Tell me more."

Tim moved behind and slipped his hands over her eyes. She breathed in and he felt her back press into his chest. He liked being close.

"Your hands smell nice," she said.

He said nothing, instead, guided her along with his hands covering her eyes and positioned her in front of the next painting. She gasped as he removed his hands to reveal the deathbed painting of Carlos Casagemas.

"Why would he paint such a thing?"

"Some say to remember a friend"
"What happened?"
"Suicide."
"Oh my God. Why?"
"The rumor is his lover rejected him...I find it fascinating that a love affair can be so full of passion that when it's gone a person's mind gets twisted to the point where they can't bear to live anymore."

"The sex must have been amazing," she said.

He felt her hands down his thighs. Simone pushed away from him and skipped ahead, turning in such a way that made him wonder what she would look like naked. *The mouse was playing with the cat.* He didn't rush up to her as she might have anticipated; instead, he strolled along toward the final piece at the end the room. Sharp sounds echoed off of the walls as Simone's heels connected with the hardwood floors. The walls closed in around them, as they approached the painting.

He crept up behind her and Simone entwined her slender fingers into his and leaned back pressing her backside into him. Her fingers were cold and dry. Their shadows danced across the white walls. Darkness filled the void around them and a sip of light washed over the painting. The guitar was positioned on the old man's frail lap, covering the length of his body. His boney fingers strummed down across the strings as his other hand fretted the chord. His ripped shirt revealed worn skin that sunk into his left shoulder. Head hunched to the right, eyes closed, and mouth open as though he had taken his final breath. Before them a macabre image of a death song played by a deceased musician.

"Why so dark?"

"You scared?"

"No... Not really, but it's kinda creepy"

"An effect the gallery devised."

The light reflecting off the painting washed over Simone's white skin, changing the tone to light blue.

"They say if you look close enough you can see a ghost in the painting."

"Ok. Well done, I'm officially freaked out!"

"What do you see?"

"What do you mean?"

"Look closer. Something is hidden within the painting." Tim said.

She took her time. Her eyes searched the painting. He noticed the whites of her eyes flash from the excitement. Realization.

"There's something hidden in the background! There, right there!" She pointed to the left hand corner of the painting. "What is it?"

"You tell me."

Simone's nose almost touched the painting she was that close. Of course, Tim knew of the hidden image within the painting. He found it years ago in a dark period of his life when all seemed lost. The finding gave him a new found love, a new sense of inspiration. It unveiled a path to deliverance. It led him to believe that something could hide underneath layers.

"It's an old woman. It's hard to make out, but I'm sure of it!"

"I have to say, Simone—I'm impressed."

"You're impressed—how do you know so much about all this?"

"When you're passionate about something it consumes you."

Tim noticed the small age lines at the corner of her eyes. He could tell she wanted to say something. Instead, she hugged him. He placed his hand on the back of her neck and pulled her closer. He moved his mouth a sliver away from her lips and stalled so he could measure her reaction. It didn't take long. Her lips moved into his, they felt soft, and her bottom lip was meaty. He liked that. This kiss lasted for the time it would take to sip a coffee, than he pulled back and stared into her eyes.

"Friends, huh," she said.

***

Tim paid for the taxi, leaving a generous tip while Simone waited for him by the revolving door to her apartment building.

They pushed through together and the moment they entered the foyer a bead of sweat trickled down his back. In the corner, a tree thrived in the humidity. Simone directed them past a guard and he attempted to wave a lazy hand at them as they moved into the hallway and up to the elevators.

Simone pressed the button lighting up the number seven. The stainless steel doors closed as he slid his hand up her leg and into the warmth between her thighs. Her hand grabbed a fistful of his shirt and they fell back into the corner. His blue-grey eyes flashed back a look of admiration at his own reflection in the mirrored back wall. He buried his head in her lush red hair. It smelled sweet, like citrus. His lips touched the skin of her neck and her heat warmed his lips. She groaned out loud as her fingernails ripped at his lower back.

She unlocked the door and they stumbled into her apartment. Tim flipped off his wet shoes and noticed a puddle forming on the cherry hardwood. In the rush to remove their jackets, they knocked a picture frame off the front hall table. The frame shattered as it hit the floor, scattering pieces of glass in all directions. He moved back against the wall transfixed by the broken frame on the floor.

"Never mind," Simone said as she pushed Tim toward the back of the apartment.

He entered the small bedroom and pushed her onto the four-poster bed that took up most of the room. It left space for one dresser and two night tables. The tables butted up against either side of the thin wood posts. Tim slid on top of her.

"Oh...Tim," Simone whispered as she bit down on his ear.

He responded in kind, taking her lobe between his teeth and bit down hard. She gasped and pulled him closer. He reached into his back pocket and slipped out the silk scarves. Tying one around her wrist, he slipped the other end around the bedpost, never losing eye contact. Simone's chest heaved and she let out another gasp.

"You're kinky...I love it." She said.

He was silent as he slipped another scarf around her free wrist. He continued the progression and tied her legs to the posts at the foot of the bed.

Her heart rocked in her chest and he felt the beat with his hands. The quick rhythm moved her large round breasts toward the ceiling as her breathing accelerated. Her red dress stretched in a v-shape and began to tear at the seams from the stress of her widespread legs.

Tim stood still, taking a moment to breathe deeply. Oxygen filled him, his heart rate slowed, his mind cleared. Looking down into Simone's eyes, he shared her want, her emotions. He admired his catch.

The mood in the room changed; the air became heavy. Simone's eyes morphed and reflected back signs of desperation. He hovered above—a moment too long, too deep and too menacing. She pulled on the scarves and winced as the silk pinched her skin.

"Come on, don't tease me."

Tim turned and walked out of the room.

"Hey! Get back here, mister!"

He took his time, exploring from room to room, while Simone called out.

In the living room, a photo album stuck out of the magazine rack. His jeans made a scraping noise as his legs shuffled. He pulled the album out and rifled through the pages. He noticed Simone in one of the photos and another woman that shared similar features. The names "Sam and Simone" written underneath in girlish handwriting. He ripped the picture from the page and returned the photo album to its original resting place.

"Tim. What are you doing?"

He said nothing.

He turned into the kitchen that was about the size of a large closet. If he spread his arms out, he could almost touch both walls. He flipped through a stack of envelopes crammed into a metal rack that hung beside the phone. A pink address book was buried in among envelopes and bills. He opened the tab that read "S" and there on the frayed paper in red ink was Sam's phone number and address. *Perfect.*

He took one last item from the kitchen before entering the bedroom.

The white skin around her ankles was red where the scarves rubbed against her skin. He ran his hand along her warm leg. She twisted, turned, and pulled at the scarves tied to her limbs. His fingers continued on their journey up her thigh and ended with his palm flat on her stomach. He felt her quivering beneath his well-manicured hand.

"Now this is more like it," she said.

He showed the address book to Simone and flipped the pages. The paper scrapping his thumb made a fluttering sound. Simone looked confused and betrayed by the introduction of the book.

"Hey, what are doing going through my stuff?"

"Ssssshhhhhhhh..." He raised his hand from her belly and pressed his index finger to his lips.

"Don't shush me. I'm serious."

"Shannon Mills, 112..."

Her body bucked hard and the scarves slipped down the posts. In one fluid motion, he pulled the long, stainless steel knife from the back of his waistband. Her eyes opened wide and her head turned away in the direction of the window. The thick, black curtains absorbed most of the light except for a sliver that gleamed off of the long blade. This seemed to quiet her and Simone's torso sank deep into her plush queen-size bed.

"I have a few rules you will need to understand."

Simone shuddered as her shoulders tightened and her fingers curled into little fists.

"Please don't...don't kill me."

"I'm glad to see that we have an understanding," he said.

TWO

Police cars sectioned off the entire block between Prince and Mott.

On Mulberry Street, the colossal bronze sculpture of Atlas faced St. Patrick's Cathedral. Across the street towers of stone laced with intricate carvings raced toward the sky, and nestled between a sign of hope, the giver of life—the Cross.

The structure stood out in the midst of the modern skyscrapers of Manhattan and added a touch of old to the twenty-first-century metropolis. Inside, the media named *Picasso Killer*, displayed his most recent victim on the sacred grounds of the oldest Catholic site in New York City.

Christine parked her unmarked Charger in behind a squad car. Manhattan natives lined the sidewalk behind the yellow tape. She searched the line of characters, and scanned each face with calmness and composure. She looked for the tell-tale-signs. That one set of eyes full of excitement, and complete admiration. Most serial killers choose their way of life because it filled a specific need. They feel a deep desire to re-live the kill. The killer, many times, will try to stay involved somehow, watching as the police unveiled their art for all to see. The experienced ones remained connected in some cases by integrating themselves in to the investigation sometimes by acting as a witness. She believes he's here amongst the crowd of spectators.

Walking up the stone staircase, she's greeted by uniformed police officers at the front entrance. Both have a look of seriousness on their faces, and the uniforms still have the out-of-the-package look. *Rookies.* She handed one of the first officers on the scene her detective's badge. He wrote down her information and pointed her inside.

The monastic interior humbled her. The full expanse of the main floor cascaded down along a sea of pews that covered the distance from the doorway to the Altar. Along the main walls, stone pillars braced the ceiling that rose to the heavens. From this distance, she couldn't distinguish the movement at the front of the cathedral as her eyes moved in and out of focus.

She walked half the distance between the front door and the Altar. Her heart pumped faster as a trickle of sweat formed on the nape of her neck. Closer now, the murder scene materialized as her eyes focused on the reflections of gold that shimmered from the skeletal steeple behind the stone Altar. Fine etching entwined along the inside frame of the structure and thin spikes ended in sharp points at the top of the facade. The victim obstructed her view of the stained-glass windows behind the gold structure. The body of a naked man hung by his limbs across the interior; a grotesque offering left behind in a place where many came to worship. She was sickened from the look of the victim's skin: overtaxed and stressed from the pulley system that held the body in position. Each rib was exposed and it reminded her of the image of Jesus nailed to the cross. An empty hole where the victim's genitalia should have been and darkness was left in its place. Chalk white skin contrasted against the man's brown, silver dollar nipples. However, the most disturbing effect left Christine shuddering; the victims head faced in the wrong direction.

Her mind wandered as she entered the mind of the killer. Thinking about the work in front of her, and the time it took to create such an unnerving spectacle. The effort and skill to slip in undetected and the patience needed to mount the horrific display. This was personal, intimate, and arrogant. Christine focused on the sheer power that it must have taken. She imagined the terror on the poor nun's face when she found the body.

Movement out of her peripheral vision interrupted Christine's thoughts. Jefferies approached and behind him, swaying toward her with the speed of a mother in her ninth month—the FBI agent.

Her Captain, William Black, had broken the news after the last murder. Michael Roberts an FBI agent out of the Manhattan office would be assisting Christine and her partner Jeffries with the Picasso case. A shot to the gut but she accepted the help only after she had exhausted all of her objections.

His black hair held tight to his scalp with gel, shone in the spotlights above the Altar. The heat from the lights showered her and she unzipped her coat.

"Christine."

"Michael," Christine said.

"Punctual this morning I see," Michael said.

Whatever.

Jefferies shook his head.

Her arms crossed her chest as she flashed Michael a look of resentment.

"You need to see the body. This is his best display so far, Picasso has really outdone himself this time," Jefferies said.

"I wish everyone would stop calling him that."

"What?" Jeffries said.

"Forget it. I take it the techs are back at the lab?" she asked.

"Yep. The pathologist has just arrived to examine the body." Jeffries said.

"Good. So, what do you have so far?"

"The cause of death is unknown, but we can assume for now that the neck injury was the fatal blow. We'll know more after the autopsy." Michael said.

"What else?"

"Well, the killer used a pulley system to mount the victim. What's interesting is that the killer tied intricate knots along the rope, which I think were more for effect, because it's clear they provide no extra function." Jeffries said.

"That's odd."

She followed Jefferies past the Altar and came to a stop in front of the victim.

"Here, look at this." Jeffries pointed to the ropes. "The ropes have an aged look to them; not worn but antique. The knots are spaced out along the rope, ten inches apart and they have a looping pattern."

"I've seen this type of knot before." Michael said

"Oh yeah, where?" she said.

"It's a sailor's knot. The actual name is "Figure of Eight." Michael said.

"What...were you a boy scout or something?" Jeffries shot.

"Unlike some of us, I actually have an education. I was sailor back in college. My team captured more than one Regatta."

"Sorry I didn't know the Skipper blessed us with his presence. Christine, what do you think should we take the three hour tour?" Jeffries asked.

"Will you two knock it off," she said. Christine shook her head in frustration. "Why do you think he picked this church?"

"You're thinking this is hate crime. Maybe the guy was a priest. Diddled a few." Jefferies said.

"I don't know. I don't see a connection between the other locations. It doesn't match up. We have a water tower in an abandoned factory, a bench in Central Park, and now this. I'm not sure what to think at this point but we should learn all we can about this one. See if there are any ties to the church. Did you find any identification?"

"Nope. Just the body." Jefferies said.

Christine turned away from the victim and looked at Michael. "Thoughts?" she asked.

"I want to go back to the first murder scene." Michael said.

"Why?" Jeffries asked.

"Need a fresh look now that we have a third crime scene."

"Sure, but it's way across the city..." Jeffries said

"So?"

"The game's on. We won't make it back in time for kick off."

"Jeffries, get your head out of your ass. The Jets don't have a chance in hell anyway!" Michael said.

They left Michael's car at the church and Christine drove them to an abandoned building banked on the Hudson River. The entire property covered ten city blocks.

She pointed to the water tower, "That's where we found her."

"Think you can make the climb?" Jefferies asked.

"What's that supposed mean?" Michael said.

She took a minute to soak in the scenery. The tower stood as a beacon among the old brick buildings. The faded logo of the Marion Wire Company blended in with rust lines that crept along the steel ladder.

"Compared to this last victim it would seem the killer's gaining some confidence." Michael said.

"I see what you mean. This place is out of the way and a closed site would have given him more time with the victim," she said.

"Wow, Michael, looks like you're breaking the stereotype," Jeffries added.

"Huh."

"FBI agents are intelligent after all." Jeffries said.

"Will you two stop fighting? Seriously," Christine said as she led them up to the base of the tower.

"After you Michael," she said.

She couldn't stomach the thought of Michael staring up at her crotch the few minutes it would take them to climb to the top.

She checked her watch. They made it to the top in exactly three minutes, Christine and Jeffries without any heavy breathing, and Michael looked like he just ran a marathon while eating chili cheese fries. He was bent at the waist, his hands rested on his knees, and he sucked air into his lungs.

She moved across the tower while sliding her hand along the chipped paint. Her fingers found the empty holes left behind by the screws that mounted the victim.

"Do you think he fixed the mounts before, or after he killed her?" Michael said.

"Not sure, but if I had to guess, I would say, before," She said.

"Why is that?"

"I think he would have cased it out first. He seems to be methodical. Not the kind of killer that would take any chances."

"True. After what he did at St Patrick's I would say he's extremely intelligent." Michael said.

"In my 20 years as a cop I've never seen anything like it. And what he did to her tits." Jeffries said.

"What do mean?" Michael asked.

"You can read it in the report and look at the photos. He removed them." Christine said.

"Matches the latest vic. I don't get that. Why remove sexual organs?" Michael said.

"Who fucking knows! It's disgusting. The guy's disturbed. The animal that did this doesn't deserve to be on the planet. These are times when I wish Manhattan still had the death penalty," she said

The view from where she stood opened up to the adjacent street. Anyone passing by could have seen the victim. For the first five blocks north, post World War II style homes with boarded-up windows lined the streets. Their roofs in great need of repair. She heard a barking dog in the distance. The trees were in skeletal form. The wind whipped around creating a thumping noise from the empty tower. She looked up at the tower in response and felt nostalgic; the tower was once the life-blood of this desolate neighborhood.

"I've seen enough. Let's head back to the station," Michael said.

"Fine with me. I'm freezing my ass off," Jeffries said.

THREE

The sun crested on the Manhattan horizon and smeared yellow-red rays through the floor to ceiling windows of Tim's condo. The rays reflected off the stainless steel vase that stood alone on the small glass table and washed his white sofa with flames of light.

Tim played his guitar. His foot tapped on the hard cherry wood floor. The muscles in his forearm relaxed with each down-strum and tightened on the up-strum. His eyes squinted as he soaked in one of the best views in Manhattan. Situated on the sixty-eighth floor, the panoramic view opened up to the Hudson River and a perfect line of sight to the Statue of Liberty.

In the living room, he sat on the edge of the brown leather sectional. He looked at the chorus of potted plants cloistered in the corner of the balcony: the weather was changing and he would have to bring them in soon.

Tim's calloused fingers plucked the strings of his Seagull acoustic. The twang of James Taylor's "Fire and Rain" rang out from the metal strings as the guitar vibrated. Together the two harmonized into the sun's rays that blanketed the wide-open room. His eyes focused on a blue, glass bottle that stood out among the others lining the shelf in the kitchen, a new addition, a token, taken from Simone's apartment during the night he raped her. His narrow view widened and he focused on the bookshelf that spread the distance between the far wall and the hallway. A Mackintosh amplifier was anchored between leather-backed books, which covered the top three rows of the oak case.

His fingers moved with a quickening pace without missing a note and the melody moved in over top of the rhythm. The music rang off of the bottles, which changed the pitch adding an eerie voicing to the song. His eyes continued trailing up the black wrought-iron spiral staircase that led up to his open bedroom loft. The dark metal railing clashed with the blue of the bottle and his vision moved in and out of focus. The blue won over and the bottle came into full view. It tugged at him.

His index finger and thumb plucked the top two strings and it sounded as if two guitars played on top of each other: the result of years of disciplined practice and bloodied fingers. He switched seamlessly from "Fire and Rain" to "How Sweet It Is to Be Loved by You." This song had different connotations for Tim than it did for some.

He played it with a rougher feel by plucking the steel strings with more intensity.

It hit him—*blue bottle*—the blue ornaments that hung on the Christmas tree like icicles in an arctic cavern and without leaving his seat, he's back home. He's with *her*.

***

He turned nine that Christmas and made something special for his mother: he wanted desperately to please her. He needed something from her, as this was the four-year anniversary of his father's death. He missed him but it seemed so long ago and the memories were fading. The cold wind whipped at his blonde hair. The tips of his fingers burned as he gripped the present. The wind continued its attack at his skin as he trekked the hundred and fifty yards from the street to the door. He wore an oversized backpack and the straps fell down his shoulders. His small hands shook as the winter wind stole the heat from his skin. The boarding school's bus dropped him off at the same time every year: December 22.

Berta met him at the door, slipped his monogrammed blazer off his shoulders, and hung it in the closet.

"How ya doin Darlin?" she said.

He shot her a forced smile as Berta straightened his hair.

"Ya know how your Mother hates a messy head. She's waitin' for ya in the livin room."

Tim picked up the present and moved along the hall.

As he walked into the expanse of the living room, he noticed *Mother* had bought a new Christmas tree. The monstrosity stood from the floor to half way up the wall and towered over Tim. Bright blue ornaments cascaded down from the white branches. Tinsel the color of mirrors showered down like rain gleaming from the overhead light, casting back reflections of his distorted image. Every few seconds, the tinsel would shift as the warm air wafted down from the brown fan above. The tree looked foreign and nothing like the real trees they used to have when his father was alive.

Mother was spread out along the black and white striped sofa. He hoped for a smile, but all he received was a quick flick of the wrist summoning him over.

"Hello Tim."

"Hi, Ann. *Mother*."

"How was the bus ride?"

"Ok I guess. I hate when we cross the bridge. It scares me."

"Don't be a wimp."

The comment stung. They always did. He noticed her eye the present but she didn't say anything about it. He took a seat beside her and felt his arm touch her bare foot. She pulled it away it response.

"I got my report card. Do you want to see it?"

She nodded. He placed the present on the seat cushion and sprinted to the front hallway. His backpack hung on the rack in the foyer. He pulled it off, unzipped the front pocket, and pulled the envelope out.

Back on the sofa, he handed the report card to his *Mother*. She was silent as she read it over. Every few seconds, her eyes would look up over the paper. There was nothing comforting in the looks. His heart pounded. She folded the report card, slipped it back into the envelope, and then tore it half. She tossed it back at him.

"I'm not paying forty-thousand a year for this level of achievement. Don't ever let me see another A-, are we clear?"

He nodded.

He picked up the two pieces of the envelope and stuck them into his pocket.

"What do you have there?"

"It's your present."

"Well...why are sitting there looking like a fool? Go and place it under the tree."

He paused for a moment, turned in his socks and walked slowly; heel toe, heel toe. He placed the present onto the floor and slid it beneath the branches. The only thing under the tree.

His sleeve caught a branch on the way up. A sudden ringing that sounded like the high pitch of rails vibrating under the extreme pressure of a freight train caused Tim to stop breathing. The ornaments clanged against one another. Trembling, he tried to silence them by placing his hand against them. This made the situation worse;

his nervous hand shook and more balls joined in the chorus. He saw it. The one lonely ball hung on the tip of a branch its hook lost hold and the ornament slipped, smashing into tiny pieces of shiny blue slivers on the floor.

Tim sucked in a deep breath. It filled his lungs and raised his small chest. The smack came faster than he anticipated, as it landed with enough force to knock him off his feet and onto the floor. His cheek stung and he felt as if a hundred pins picked at his soft skin.

"You ass. You clumsy retard. Look what you did!"

Tim looked up into his Mother's angry face. Her skin blotched with spots of red. Her black silk nightgown matched the way he felt.

"Berta! Berta, get in here!"

Berta arrived within seconds. Tim watched as Berta's eyes moved from the mess to his mother and back to him. Her look of concern couldn't extinguish the embarrassment he felt. His chin fell to his chest and a single tear crept out from the corner of his eye, which he wiped with the sleeve of his shirt.

"Are you crying? Those better not be tears," Ann said. She pointed toward the door.

He knew what that meant and followed her direction. Tim pushed himself off of the floor and scurried out of the room.

He passed Berta on the way out. Their arms brushed and her skin felt warm. He scrambled to control the turmoil of emotions that thrashed inside of him.

The stairs felt mountainous. Each step squeezed the breath from him, which made the hike a slow one.

"Clean every last speck. I don't want one reminder of what that little bastard did. You understand?" Ann commanded.

The orders spewed through the open doors of the living room and rushed up the stairs like fast moving flames searching for oxygen. His thoughts turned to anger and he slammed his fist into the railing. The vibration pulsated up his arm, and what felt like an army of ants below the surface of his skin, raced along behind and bit at the meaty part of his hand.

***

The ringing of the guitar strings pulled at him as the melody woke him from his trance. He palmed the strings and muted the sound. He rose from the sofa and placed the guitar back in the safety of the hook on the wall. There it stood alone, amongst the sea of glass windows glimmering like a mirage. He thought of Ann and then of Simone and a smile formed across his face.

FOUR

Simone's breathing was a mere whisper among the intrusive sounds of horns that shrieked through the window as she curled into her duvet. Creases in the fabric pressed beneath her, which created a sea of miniature mountain ranges atop the oversized fabric. Her skin looked a shade darker compared to the bright waves of white on her queen-size bed and the remains of the red dress beneath her resembled a pool of blood among the ocean of white silk-polyester blend.

Simone's distant eyes froze in a long-drawn-out-gaze. Her shoulders hunched inward, her arms extended across the folds of the pillow, ending with her hands together and her fingers entwined in full prayer. Her two-hundred dollar hairstyle flung around her face in a mess of red.

The memory of the prior night's events scattered like bits of debris that whipped through the air from a category five tornado. Simone tried to pull the pieces back together and play them back over and over. She reminisced. Tim's smile. The way he held her on the train. She would have given herself to him willingly but what he did left her breathless. She wanted him... he didn't have to rape her, but the sex was fantastic. She couldn't discount that. It was the first time she had ever acted out a rape and he was convincing. She went along with it and played the part of the victim like Jody Foster in "The Accused".

Most women after such brutalization would be lost in their internal sorrow. The confusion would set in and plant roots, turning the woman inward. The sickening and the doubt would eat away at their souls and a metamorphosis would occur changing that once innocent bright life that was full of optimism to one of a darker shade. But that was most women—and not Simone. Because in order to keep the night in check, she had to believe that it was an act. She found it odd that he cleaned her apartment afterwards: wiping down the bed, vacuuming, and the whole time an orange citrus smell lingered. Some sort of fetish she guessed.

The buzzing of her cell phone spanked her out of her thoughts. She reached for it on the nightstand. It wasn't there. *Work... Shit! Shit!*

She scrambled off the bed and moved clumsily out of the room to the kitchen. The counter was empty: no purse. She ran into the hallway. The hardwood slapped against her bare feet. She remembers...too late.

The sharp pieces of glass slid into the bottoms of her feet. Shooting pain caused her knees to give, folding her like a lawn chair. She crashed to the floor elbow first, jamming her fist into her ribs. The force of the blow sucked the wind out of her. *Why didn't he clean that?*

Lying in pain against the cold wood floor, she reached under the table and slid her purse off the vent and into her arms. The warm leather felt strange against her bare breasts. Her fingers fumbled with the clasp and with a little struggle, she opened it. Naked on the floor among the shattered pieces of glass she answered her phone.

"It's Simone."

Carl spoke in a direct tone, "Where the hell are you?"

"Carl, I won't be in today. I'm not feeling well."

"Ok."

Without another response, the call ended.

In the comfort of her bed, she removed the last shards of glass and bandaged her feet.

She looked around the room. It was cleaner than usual other than her bed, which was still unmade. She noticed the scarves that still hung from the bedposts. They were a reminder of him. The thick drapes blocked the world outside. The picture of her and her sister, left behind as a reminder of his rules. His rules etched in her mind like the branding on new cattle. She liked his game.

A lullaby whispered in her ear and sung the mystic song of the sandman. She slept.

FIVE

Tim moved among the streams of litter on the pavement. He kicked an empty coffee cup. He took care not to scuff his Steve Maddens as he flipped the cup over and slid it into the gutter. A discarded fold of the Times flapped against the light post on the corner of 72nd and Amsterdam. A neon sign flashed *Café Bar* on the building beside him. He took notice of the flickering florescent tubes and wondered why this was the first time since following Christine the sign had caught his eye.

She lived down the corner in a small, seven-story building. She must be running late today, or possibly, she left early. Either way, their paths would cross again. For now, Simone would soothe his needs because Christine was his special project: one he wouldn't rush.

Across the street native New Yorkers jammed into the subway entrance at Verdi Square. A woman stopped beside him and looked up at him. She could have passed for a young girl except for the thick lines on her face. He thought of raisins. She stared so deep it felt like a violation. *You see me, don't you old woman.* Then her lips parted, a row of yellow teeth flashed back, and her face softened as she smiled up at him.

The light turned red, the oncoming traffic halted, and the white pedestrian glowed from the LEDs. He took the woman's arm and escorted her across the street.

As they stepped up onto the opposite sidewalk, she thanked him by revealing the Marlboro yellows once again and left in the direction of the subway doors.

The woman stuck in his mind and reminded him of a life near its end. Life had a way of delivering unexpected twists and turns. Some experiences taught hard lessons and sometimes changed a person. And for Tim, his life-lessons blackened his heart, which pumped blood filled with anger and resentment. His life he controlled; and in the world he lived in, he took what was rightfully his. His outcome would never be left up to fate.

Losing his father early in his childhood was a blessing in disguise because it allowed his mother the time to ingrain in him a true sense of morality. A lesson he would cherish and more than likely take to his grave.

Funny thing, fate. Simone may not know it now, but her decision to save her hair from the rain, and venture into Starbucks would change her life forever. She put on a terrific show. She revealed more than necessary, all in an effort to capture the attention most women like her longed for. *Why would they put themselves on display like that? Why the fake breasts, waxed legs, and the Botox?* He longed for originality and these types of women were scattered throughout Manhattan like sawdust in a lumber mill.

Christine was different and this is why he took his time with her. He liked how, on most days, she didn't wear make-up and revealed nothing of herself sexually. He had tracked her for the past five months and he would continue tracking for five more until the time was right.

The pavement slapped back against the wood soles of his shoes as he ambled down the sidewalk on 72nd Street. He scanned each face as they passed.

Don't you see me?

Look at me! I'm a killer!

I'm going to kill again!

None would hear his thoughts; none would see him. If they only looked deep into his eyes and drank from his soul, then they would know the terror that he was capable of inflicting.

He managed to get the attention of a young man. His hair was slick with goop and the ends stuck up in the shape of a fan. He believed they called that style a faux-hawk.

You.

You do it.

Look at me. See me.

Oh, you see me. Don't you?

Don't you want to stop me?
Nothing.
The man walked past with a quick glance. He actually smiled. It was warm and courteous.
Not today, huh?
Ok. No problem. Another time then.
Simone would be where he left her in the late hours of the morning. In his experience, over the years with women like Simone, there were only two possible outcomes: either she could be controlled or she would be killed.

SIX

Christine entered the briefing room and the light from the overhead fluorescents lit up the space. She squinted from the glare that came off of the white concrete walls. Her eyes adjusted to the light as she scanned the room. Michael took a seat at the end of the table. He had the chair turned around so that his arms rested on the back. His rolled up sleeves revealed a jungle of hair. The image reminded Christine of the gorilla costume her father wore one Halloween.

Two white boards lined the back wall and displayed pictures of the crime scenes from St. Patrick's Cathedral, Marion Wire Company's water tower and the bench at Central Park. Crystal, one of the techs stood alongside Jeffries at the end of the room.

Crystal broke the silence. "We didn't find any hair or fingerprints on the body. The victim was male, forty-three, with blonde hair and a tanned complexion. The cause of death was a dislodged cervical vertebra. There was a loss of nerve supply to the body. The victim suffered a sudden and extreme drop in blood pressure, which lead to a quick death. The medical examiner noted that both arms were, in fact, broken during the struggle."

"Were you able to identify the victim?" Christine asked.

Michael said nothing.

Christine accepted the file from Crystal and the tech tucked her short blonde hair behind her ears. When Christine looked in to Crystal's eyes, she saw an honest person. She liked Crystal. She worked hard.

"No. We checked dental records and ran his fingerprints. No hits yet. We've sent his photo around to missing persons and we hope to hear back soon. We do know the victim wasn't killed in the church though," Crystal said.

"This is a detailed report and so far so good. Nevertheless, I find it hard to believe that the victim was not killed at St. Patrick's," Michael said.

Crystal looked like she was pondering Michael's comment. "We know the killer cleaned the body before he brought it to the church. We found traces of commercial grade soap in both his hair and on his skin and we found no trace of this at the church," Crystal said.

Michael coughed out as if he was clearing his throat. Christine thought the guy was in over his head.

"I was able to link an oily substance to each of the vics in the prior cases, all the bodies were cleaned, but we always found this strange oily residue embedded in the epidermis around their ankles. After running the analysis, we found the oil came from leather. I ran that type of leather against the data base samples and we came back with a hit. This type of leather's used to make cuffs: Bondage Restraints."

"Really? So our perps into S&M?" Michael said.

"We don't think so."

"Good thing you're paid to analyze and not to think," Michael said.

Christine watched as Crystal took the full brunt of the comment and wondered why Michael was such a prick.

"We think the killer used the restraints to hang the victims from their ankles. After checking the report again it showed that there were clear ligature marks on all the vics," said Crystal.

"Why would he do that? Any thoughts?" Christine asked.

"To wash them. The post mortem report confirmed it. Based on the coagulation direction of the blood the victims were indeed killed while hanging upside down," Crystal added.

"Makes sense." Christine said.

"The problem is this type of leather is used to make many types of restraints so we can't pinpoint it down to one specific brand. But if we find the original pair we can try to compare that to our sample and hopefully there's some DNA to go along with it."

"Ok. What else?" Christine asked.

"The pathologist's report stated that from the vic's temperatures they were all killed within eighteen hours of the staging. That means that based on the crime scene locations, the primary crime scenes would have to be somewhere close, considering the time it would have taken to arrange the bodies. I have plotted a geographical map of where we found all three. You can see for yourself."

Christine watched Crystal as she pointed out the location on the map on the corkboard.

"The initial crime scene is here somewhere in Manhattan."

"There's more. Each victim also had traces of Polyethylene Glycol that coated their eyes. We think he used this to keep the eyelids open. This would leave a surprised look on the victim's faces."

"It looks like the killer's motivation is hedonistic. It seems to be more about the thrill, the hunt, and the display." Michael said.

"Have you linked the Glycol or whatever you call it?" Jeffries asked.

"The wax is commonly used in the food industry. It's used as a coating for fruits and vegetables." Crystal said.

"Ok, now we're getting somewhere. Do we have a list of industries that use this wax, or distribute it?" Christine asked.

"No but I'll get right on it." Crystal said.

"We did find something unusual about the rope used to hang him to the archway. The rope is made of hemp. It's old. We received the results. It's weird."

"Why, did you smoke some of it?" Michael said.

Christine observed Michael laughing and was not amused.

"Continue, Crystal," Christine said.

"The rope dates back to ancient Egypt. The Egyptians used ropes made from hemp fiber: Cannabis sativa. The rope could bear three tons or more if braided together. The Egyptians used the rope on a pulley system to move massive slabs of rock. Like I said, weird huh?"

Christine found the last detail about the rope interesting; she wondered how many ropes of that type would be traceable. They must be a collector's item, or museum artifact.

"Crystal, this is a good lead. Run with it. Generate a database of collectors and museums that have access to this kind of rope."

"You got it!" Crystal said.

Time became the enemy and stole away the minutes of the day. She needed rest. Each day held only so many hours. This was her second day without sleep. Her mind, fueled with caffeine, screamed for some shuteye.

The rope was a good lead and the best one so far. She'd have to brief the Captain tomorrow.

"All right everyone, go and get some rest. We have a big day tomorrow. The press will be all over us in the morning." Christine said.

Christine left them all standing in the room.

***

Christine arrived home at 1:15am. The drive was uneventful and, at this time in the morning, the only people on the streets were either prostitutes or drug addicts. That wasn't her division.

After unlocking her apartment door Christine placed her gun and badge on the hallway table alongside her keys. She hung up her coat in the closet.

After a day like today, Christine did not open a bottle of wine. Instead, she headed straight for her liquor cabinet and poured herself a double of Crown Royal mixed with a splash of Diet Coke.

Christine swallowed the last of her drink. She felt the warmth of the whiskey coat her stomach and relished the burn.

In the bathroom, she turned on the shower and checked the temperature. Tonight she needed it hot.

She undressed. Her clothes beneath her in a pile. She entered the shower and felt the heat of the water attack her skin.

In the shower, she could escape the day if only for a few minutes and she took her time. The water soaked her hair, which clung to her back, face, and neck. The steam filled the room while rivers of water flowed their way down the curves of her hard body. The currents twisted and turned navigating around her ample breasts, flowing down the small of her back. Her long legs showed lots of definition from relentless time spent at the gym and she lathered the white foam down them with a sense of accomplishment.

She washed her hair taking time to pull the long black strands to the left of her face and lathered, first with shampoo, then conditioner. She squeezed out the body wash from the plastic bottle and cleaned herself thoroughly washing away the filth of the day.

Turning off the shower, she put on her robe and walked into her bedroom. Tonight she was too exhausted to wait for her hair to dry. She set her alarm, turned off the light, and slept.

SEVEN

Tim knocked on the door. He could see the eyehole flash dark then light again. The lock disengaged and the apartment door opened. He knew it would.

Simone's wet hair clung to her face. Her eyes pierced his and lingered as he expected. He understood her type and he'd seen many before—the broken ones.

Tim pushed Simone back into the apartment and shut the door behind him. She stood before him. Her silk robe opened down her front covering her breasts but exposing her white cotton panties. She didn't bother to cover up, but, instead, turned and walked toward the living room. Tim followed. She sat cross-legged on the sofa. Tim sat beside her. He reached out and pulled her hand into his own.

"You look like shit," he said.

"Nice...thanks for the compliment."

"You should have applied lipstick on those beautiful lips."

"Who would I need to do that for?"

"Me! You're not happy that I'm here?"

"Huh! After that comment?"

"Don't lose sight of what's important."

Simone's eyes shifted off and up to the right. Her lip curled up and to the right as well. Her shoulders collapsed back into the soft cushions.

"So you do that with all the girls you fuck?"

Tim stared back with composure and with control.

"I like you like this," he said.

"Like what?"

Tim slid his hand down her arm and cupped her elbow. With the back of his other hand, he brushed her cheek softly, slowly. Tim's hand stopped and rested on the back of her head. He wove strands of her wet hair between his fingers. Her head reluctantly fell into his palm. She let out the breath that she held. He would break her easier than most. For some it took days but not Simone. He could tell from the moment that he saw her in the café that she was special: a broken one. Most men would take one look at Simone and lose all self-confidence because of the way she looked. Tim zeroed in on the subtleties. It was pouring rain and instead of wearing suitable attire for the climate, she wore a scandalous red dress.

"I like that you passed my test. You've proven yourself. We can now move to the next level."

"What the fuck does that mean?"

"Get dressed."

Surprising to her, he was sure, but not surprising to Tim, she got up.

"What am I changing into?"

Everything and anything I want you to.

"Something sexy...I'll meet you downstairs."

***

Tim gripped the wheel of his Audi. The soft hum of the powerful V6 vibrated the leather interior. The green glow from the console changed his blue-grey eyes to aquamarine as he looked into the review mirror.

Simone swung through the revolving doors. She looked revitalized and twirled as she approached the sedan. Tim slid across the seat and opened the passenger side door. Cool autumn air mixed with the warm air blowing through the vents. The seat warmer was too hot underneath him. He pressed the button on the console to turn it down. His leather glove washed over the gearshift, his hand and the leather knob formed a union of cowhide. Simone's white dress covered almost nothing. A black, mink bolero wrapped her shoulders.

Tim released the clutch and the force pulled them both deep into their leather bucket seats. The Audi clawed the pavement racing down Columbus, weaving in and out of the lines of yellow cabs. A sharp right on 70th, and they sped between parked cars that lined both sides of the street. One flinch on the wheel and sparks would light up the night. Lincoln Towers flashed by as they cornered onto Freedom Place. Without a second to breathe, they cornered left on 66th then right onto 11th Avenue. Simone's hand pressed down hard on Tim's leg and her fingernails bit through his Hugo Boss pants, leaving behind nail marks.

Tim pulled the car into the valet parking at the Marquee. Even on a Tuesday night, the line-up rounded the corner. One line for VIP's, another full of chumps waiting with hopes of getting in. They never did. Models from the fashion district filled the VIP line. They wore clothing that reminded him of dental floss. Latin music spilled out of the doors and through the bouncer's thick chest.

The valet took the keys, and pocketed a fifty as well. Tim opened the passenger door for Simone. Her long, milky-white legs extended out and anyone with the right angle could see her in all her glory.

Tim walked up to a security guard, who thumbed at a Blackberry and Tim whispered into his ear. An escort, summoned by the guard, ushered them into the club. Once inside, the pressure filled him. Bass boomed, as the music pumped through the speakers. It engulfed him. The sensation reminded him of scuba diving at 60 feet below sea level.

The host placed them at a booth alongside a group of models at the left corner of the bar. Martini glasses filled the table—a drink Tim would never place in his hand. Simone slid in beside an Asian woman, who made her look obese in comparison. *Eat something.*

Before they could settle in, a frosted lowball of Crown Royal smothered a napkin with a Marquee logo.

"...and for you baby?" asked the waitress.

"She'll have an apple martini... make it a double," said Tim.

Tim watched as the server, with a tight ass and small tits, scurried away.

Tim's eyes fell to the anorexic Asian beside Simone. The gold dress hung off her as if it would blow away with the slightest breeze. The opening at the side provided a clear view of a small, firm breast that bounced in rhythm with the bass pounding out of the speakers. He counted her ribs, one by one. As if she felt his gaze, she turned her head and her dark-lined eyes returned a seductive glance. Tim smiled at the thin woman and in his peripheral caught Simone's reaction. Tim felt Simone's hand shoot to his knee.

The server returned with a large martini glass topped with a slice of Granny Smith. Simone swallowed the contents and ordered another before the server had a chance to turn away.

Tim whispered into Simone's ear and then bit down on her lobe. She looked back with a shy expression on her face. Tim nodded with a look of encouragement. Without further hesitation, Simone slipped her hand beneath the Asian's dress and cupped her round breast.

In a fluid motion, the woman turned toward Simone. Not angry, not surprised, but hungry. Their eyes locked and smirks lined both the women's faces, while the Latin samba melodies bounced around the room. Tim moved aside to let the two playmates out of the booth.

Clubbers filled the small dance floor. All of them moving to the same rhythm. A cloud of mystery hung low in the room. Tim watched all the bodies brushing and thought that the regulars checked their jackets, along with their morality, at the coat check.

Simone led the woman up to the dance floor, pulled the woman in against her as their hips swayed to the beat. Legs overlapped, hands explored, and hair touched. The seductive Latin melody showered over the girls and they looked intoxicated by the rhythm.

Tim felt alive, enthralled, and in control of the situation. He created this event. And he was proud of how Simone was coming along. He followed a system, which he created through years of practice. Every nuance in his voice, the way he styled his hair, manicured his nails; the hours spent perfecting the pitch of his voice. He had to learn everything he could about women. He read their magazines. He asked them questions and listened to their answers. He studied their movements and looked for what the body language revealed that their answers didn't. It's been a long tedious experience but now as he stared at his puppet grinding against the Asian, he knew the craft was perfected.

The song ended and the marionettes unglued. They moved back toward the table and Tim rose to make room for them.

The martini waited patiently for Simone. Beads of water defrosted down the glass and soaked the napkin below.

Tim studied Simone as she emptied the contents of the glass into her mouth. Redness filled her white cheeks and glowed from her throat. She reached over to him and, with the tips of her fingers, feverishly rubbed his chest. Simone pinched his nipple and he felt her hunger through her touch.

"Get her number," he said

"Really?"

"I like how you look with her. It's hot. Maybe a plaything for you...later," he said.

Her eyes narrowed and her lips spread into a thin line.

Simone nodded, whispered into the woman's ear, and flicked at her cheek with the tip of her tongue. Tim watched with a sense of accomplishment as the two discussed the details. Simone entered the woman's number into her cell phone.

Tim seized Simone's hand in his and stood up from the leather bench. Her eyes lit with excitement as she followed without resistance, like butter melting in the middle of a hot pan.

The Audi waited at the curb. Tim poured Simone into the passenger seat, closing the door. The air felt crisp and electrifying. The lights from the building outside reminded him of the needless energy wasted in the city.

The Audi came to an abrupt stop outside Simone's building. Tim turned to Simone; desire filled her eyes.

"Get out."

Her eyes changed as soon as the words hit home. The ravenous expression turned to one of wonderment and one of confusion—lost.

"You heard me...get out."

Without objection or defense, Simone turned and opened the car door.

"Will I see you again?"

"Soon...if you're good."

Tim applied pressure on the accelerator before the door had time to seal the world out.

EIGHT

Tim sat his desk. The glass top reflected the sun's rays as he flipped through the pictures of Christine. Her confidence exuded from the photo. It was the intransigent aura about her. The way she held her coffee cup. Her posture. She looked people in the eye during conversation. He noticed her picture in an online article ten months ago. Detective Christine Maloan was the lead detective in a serial murder case. He said her name aloud that day as he read the journalist's rendition of the story and even her name—as it echoed in his ears—held a commanding tone.

He looked her up. She wasn't hard to find. Thanks to the media, he knew the precinct she worked out of. Once he wandered into her precinct. She was there. He told the officer at the front desk that he wrote crime novels and he wanted to get a feeling for the atmosphere. He wasn't given freedom to move around at will, instead, he received a guided tour and that was the first time he saw her in the flesh.

He followed her almost every week after that. Sometimes he would skip a week to avoid repetition; although he was skilled at the craft, he knew that eventually she would take notice if he didn't break the pattern and those days he would amuse himself with the others. There was never just one.

Three months into the exploration, he had her patterns down to a consistent schedule. Coffee every morning at Starbuck on 72nd. The gym every Tuesday, Thursday, and Sunday; sometimes alternating morning and evening workouts. He watched once within an arms distance. He typed into his Blackberry taking notes of what he experienced and blended in with the rest of Manhattan's communication junkies. He could smell her sweat. He noted the scent. It was strong but not pungent and he liked that. Her hair was tied in a ponytail and the thick black tress swayed from side to side as they moved down the sidewalk.

Another time she entered her apartment building and stopped in an act of kindness to open the door for a man. He smiled at her as he walked out of the building. Their arms brushed. Tim felt a wave of envy.

The thought of nostalgia faded as he placed the photos back into the folder. He slid the folder that contained all the information he gathered on Christine back into its place in the steel meshed desk-organizer.

He locked his door and took the elevator to the lobby.

Outside, he entered the subway station on West Broadway and took the A train to the Upper West Side.

***

One small glass of orange juice, one egg, and one piece of brown toast mixed in her stomach as Christine pushed out the front door of her building. She headed toward Starbucks just the right amount of distance to kick-start her metabolism.

After ten months, the leads were finally starting to fit together. Today she would spend the day combing through the evidence again. Something would jump out. It always did.

She rounded the corner of seventy-second and passed through Verdi Square. Suits and skirts moved in the direction of the subway entrance brushing fabric as the worker bees moved through the doors. Christine walked past them with authority. She rounded the corner on 72nd and the green sign caught her eye. *My friend.*

One person stood at the cashier. This was an unusual sight and gave her another ten minutes in her day. She might even make it to work early.

The skinny vanilla latte warmed her hand as she pushed through the door. She had her head down for only a second, yet the impact happened anyway. She tried to swing around him with a maneuver that came from basic training, too late. The coffee cup crushed in her hand. An explosion of white foam covered his brown suede coat and her black suit jacket. Together they looked like a s' more melted from the heat of a campfire. They looked at each other for the longest time. Finally, the tension broke with a loud deep belly laugh from Christine. She looked into his blue-grey eyes and smiled flashing him a sea of white.

"I'm so sorry," she said.

Another laugh slipped out and he began to laugh as well.

"It's ok..."

She studied him as he reached inside his coat and pulled out a handkerchief. He wiped the foamy mess from his jacket, leaving a dark wet streak in the suede. Then he handed her the cloth.

"I figured you would want to do this yourself," he said.

"A true gentleman in Manhattan. You're one in a million."

She wiped off her jacket and tried to hand the cloth back to him. He raised both hands and stopped her.

"You better keep that. You never know when you might need it again."

Christine laughed. "Hey!"

He picked up the empty cup and handed it back to her.

"I can't believe how clumsy I am."

"Please don't worry about; it's ok really," he said.

"You have to let me pay for the dry cleaning,"

"No. It's ok, really."

"No, I insist. Please, here's my card. Send me the bill."

"Ok. But only if you let me buy you another coffee."

She looked at her watch. She had at least ten extra minutes to kill.

"Why not."

"Hi, I'm Tim…"

She waited patiently as he gazed over the card.

"…and you're Detective Maloan," he added.

Christine saw his extended hand and shook it.

***

Christine marched up the four steps that led up to the front entrance of the precinct. The door opened and she almost knocked into Jefferies. *What's with me today?*

"Hey Christine. In a hurry?"

"Sorry."

"I was just looking for you."

"Oh yeah, why's that?"

"I just got off the phone with Crystal and it seems were about to make some serious headway with the Picasso case."

"Really?"

"You bet."

"Great! What did she find?"

"A chemical lead."

She listened while Jeffries explained the new lead and as he trailed off, she remembered what she wanted to tell him.

"Listen, Teresa called me. You need to talk to her," she said.

"What are you? My marriage counselor now?"

"Hey. Don't do that."

"Do what?

"Dodge the comment, that's what. Honestly I like your wife; but I'm getting tired of the phone calls..."

"Well, she shouldn't be calling you. Just forget it. I'll deal with her."

"Well, do it soon. Cause she sounds like she's fed up." Christine said.

"As soon as I close this case, I'll take her and Jenny on a vacation that will shut her up."

"Do you hear yourself?" She shook her head and was surprised by his comment. "Taking them on a vacation may fix things in the short term. You need to open up... and change your attitude," she said.

"Sure, sounds good. Whatever. Let's go see Crystal."

"Fine"

Christine and Jeffries walked into the lab, as Crystal scanned a piece of evidence with a purple light. She looked cute with her orange glasses on. The tech had a fine mist of sweat across her bro. The heat from the noisy vent above blasted down hot air.

"Hey you, I hear you have news for me," she said.

"Christine! I'm so glad you're here. Look at this." Crystal said as she slipped off the glasses and clicked off the purple light.

Crystal waved her over. She showed her a list. It contained a group of companies that distributed Polyethylene Glycol. She highlighted a Manhattan company, Zosma Imports.

"I like this one," Crystal said.

"Why?"

"The company's based out of Manhattan. They have a warehouse on the Hudson River just off Twelfth Street, near the Jacob Javits Center. The owner is James Lawson—his company holds the distribution rights for all of North America."

"How do you know this?"

"The producer of the wax is a chemical manufacturing company based in China. They faxed over the documents today."

Christine smiled at the tech. She was really proving to be a great asset.

"Good job." Christine said. "Alright, what else did you find out?"

"I ran down the rope leads. Turns out that there were only eight sets of Egyptian ropes left worldwide; six are in museums and two are with collectors. Guess who owns a set of these ropes?"

"James Lawson."

"You got it. I found a press release online that states that he purchased this ten years ago. Amazing what you can Google these days."

"This is good news. This should be enough for a search warrant."

NINE

As he pressed down the accelerator, he thought of the encounter with Christine and was elated. His timing was perfect. She even thought it was her fault. He loved that. The seed was planted and now he would give it time to grow. It was different watching her from a distance but up close and engaged felt amazing and something about her eyes ignited his pilot light.

The wind whistled through the opening in the driver side window and ruffled his hair. The bass pounded his leather seat. He tapped the steering wheel in rhythm along with 'Black Betty' as the music radiated from the five-point-one Bose Surround System. Tim pushed a little harder. The front of the Audi pulled up and the car sped forward. The back of another car moved closer into his vision like an apparition. He moved his hand onto the gearshift, dropped it into third, and stomped onto the pedal. The engine whined as he moved into the oncoming lane.

The Toyota looked like a spec in the review mirror as he roared past. The forest engulfed him as the vehicle sped along Hwy 87. The power of the sedan thrilled him and he respected the machine. He thumbed the MP3 player's control on the steering wheel and skipped ahead to the next song. Without another car in sight, "Paralyzer" generated an ominous ambiance that filled the interior. He fingered the power window switch and the car sealed, closing out the world.

Visions of Christine filled him as he reminisced. Then he had it. He remembered. It was her dark hair, high cheekbones and her fair skin. The way her dimpled chin came down to a point. Christine's top lip was as thick as the bottom—plump. Her eyes looked angry and yet beautiful. A mystery. A jewel. Christine's deep emerald green eyes were a perfect match to Ann's.

Then the song ended and "I'll Keep Your Memory Vague" escaped from the speakers. The smooth acoustic strumming and Scott Anderson's liquid-sandy voice, along with the thoughts of his Mother, darkened Tim's mood.

Ann.

***

Alone in his room he stared at the stain on his white shirt. The stain caused by the tears. He felt numb, closed off, and unconscious to the knocking at his door.

The door opened and Berta stood in the doorway. She had a concerned look on her face and at the same time a flicker of sadness. Tim could tell that she pitied him.

"Hey there. How ya doin?"

Tim didn't respond. He sat there on his bed with his back straight, and his hands folded in his lap. Wearing the clothes from yesterday.

"Your mother wants to see ya."

"You mean Ann."

Her pudgy cheeks drooped and her mouth turned down at the sides.

"Let's get you dressed. Ok hun."

Tim stood up bending at the knees. His hands never touched the bed. Berta walked over to the dresser. Pulled out plain white briefs and a pair of socks.

She laid them on the bed beside him. She moved quicker now. Into the closet and returned with a button down polo shirt and wool sweater in one hand. In her other, a pair of brown khaki pants. The crease stood out on the leg as she placed the clothes on the bed as well.

"You need to get dressed now hun. Ok?"

He gripped the cold hardwood railing and he pulled his hand away in reaction to the temperature. The carpet cushioned each step he took as he made the hike down the staircase. He felt small in comparison to the house. The snapping and biting sounds of the wood burning in the fireplace terrified him. The flames ate into the wood, the fire hissed; Tim dreaded the encounter, not with the fire—with Ann.

He missed his father. The memory of him lingered like an outline hidden behind a fog. Death came for him too soon. He prayed to God for his father's return—another unanswered prayer.

A snap came from the room in front of him. He turned the corner and there she was.

She stood with her back to him. Her long torso ended at the nape of her neck. Her thick shiny black hair was pulled into a ponytail and tucked loosely over her left shoulder. She turned and her ponytail swung off her shoulder and vanished behind her back. He thought she looked pretty.

She smiled sometimes, but her eyes were always distant. Today she wasn't smiling. He was careful not to stare for too long. Those green eyes delivered pain.

"Tim, come over here and take a seat on the sofa."

Tim did as she directed and moved to the sofa. The cushions were warm from the fire and comforted him as he sat with perfect posture. His hands were folded in his lap.

He gazed at her as she crossed in front of him. Her long legs slid past one another underneath her black dress and made a soft whispering noise. She bent down and picked up the present from the floor, graceful not one branch stirred, not one ball moved.

"Is this my Christmas present Tim?"

"Yes, I hope you like it."

She smiled and slid one long French manicured nail along the edge. The tip fell in behind the festive wrapping and a slight tear opened in the corner.

"Aren't you going to wait until Christmas?"

She ripped the paper off the box. Her smile faded and her eyes darkened. The light from the fire flickered in them. Her hand moved quickly, removing the rest of the paper. She threw the wrapping to the floor. The box looked small in her hands compared to when he had held it. The white cardboard flashed orange as the fire spat behind him.

She opened the lid and removed the contents, handing him the box. He held it tight to his chest. She towered over him, staring at the glass frame.

"Where did you get this?"

"The store on campus. Do you like it?"

Her fingers picked at the artificial snowflakes that lined the frame. One of the flakes fell off and landed on the discarded paper on the floor below her.

"Do you miss your father?"

"I do. I miss him very much. That's the picture I had at school. The only one with all of us. Before..."

"Before he died. Is that what you were going to say?

Tim's eyes shot to his socks and focused on the white cotton. "Yes."

"Look at me," she said.

She turned the photo toward him. The tall evergreens surrounded a small house. Their branches dipped from the weight of the snow covered tips. Smoke rose from the short brick chimney. White puffs of smoke in the shape of snowflakes floated up into the night sky. Warm light shone from the two front windows framed in a cross pattern. In front of the house, he stood between his mother and father holding their hands.

Her eyes met his. He waited for it. It never came. She hadn't smiled at all, no kiss on the cheek. *He hoped.*

"Do you like it?"

"Tim. You want to know what I think?"

"Yes, I hope you really like. Do you like it?

She flipped the picture between her fingers. Tim could see the light reflect off the glass. The house became blurry. The trees became blurry. The frame rested between her fingertips and her thumb. Her hand moved in an up and down motion. His mind was sharp. His eyes glued to the picture of his family resting on the tips of her fingers. He looked from the frame to her eyes. They were squinting. She smirked.

"Mother...it's going to fall..."

Nothing.

"Ann, it's going to fall..."

She released it and let it drop. He reached out and it was an inch too far. The image of his once happy family shattered on the floor at her feet.

The plastic back held the torn picture. Sharp edges replaced the winter snowflakes. The image of the winter home was now a crime scene with the evidence of the destruction, in pieces, in front of him, and the criminal was not running. Not hiding, but towering over him—smiling.

"Now we're even."

She turned and walked in long strides out of the room passing Berta in the doorway.

"Don't you dare clean that up. Let him."

***

Tim turned onto Aimers Road from Country Route 42. The Audi managed the steep climb without resistance as he navigated the winding road to his cabin. He pulled into the driveway and the modern wood structure stood out amongst the aged mountainside. The straight lines squared off on the ends and all sides met at the top of the flat roof. Light glowed through the wood slats in the window. He shut off the engine and the car slept. He opened the driver side door, breaking the seal, and the warm air mixed with the cool mountain air.

The strength of the mountain invigorated him. He took a deep breath and the clean air filled his lungs. He treasured the way the evergreens smelled. Pine needles discarded from their wooden mothers were soft under his shoes.

He loved it here. It was majestic. It was the first home he had built with his inheritance and it was perfect.

Inside the lobby, she met up with Jeffries and Michael. They were chatting up a leggy brunette.

"You must be detective Maloan? I'm Katie. Lawson's Executive Assistant."

"Yes. And I see you have already met my partners," she said.

"Yes, very funny men, these two. Please follow me; the elevator is this way," she said and waved to them as she turned. "Zosma Imports has its own private elevator. It's around back."

Long toned legs squeezed out from beneath the receptionist's tight skirt and as she turned, Christine could see through her white shirt. She could make out the full shape of her breasts. Katie wasn't wearing a bra. Christine was disgusted. She looked over at Michael. He was leering.

Smiling back at them, the receptionist motioned them to follow her. They did. She scanned her card on the black plate on the wall and the elevator doors opened. They stood behind the receptionist and she touched the only button on the panel. It was a stainless steel logo, 'Zosma'. Michael's eyes never moved off the receptionist's backside the whole thirty-five seconds it took to reach the top floor.

The elevator opened to a large reception area. A steel sign on the back wall sported 'Zosma Inc.' and underneath, in large, black wrought iron 'A Division Of Lawson Industries'. In front of the sign was a large oak

TEN

The car idled in the line of traffic. Christine looked ahead at the yellow cab. The sign on the roof advertised a new Broadway play "Wicked". She thought of Dorothy from the Wizard of Oz, her freckled cheeks and silky voice.

"So he agreed to see us just like that?" Michael asked.

"Yep, he was extremely courteous. Said he would do all he could to help," she said.

"No shit." Michael said.

"Why are you surprised? Are you assuming this guy's guilty already, Michael?" Jeffries asked.

Christine inched the Charger through the intersection and stopped again on the other side.

Twenty minutes later, she pulled up to the front entrance of 405 Park Ave. She let Jeffries and Michael out, and drove off to find parking.

desk with pewter trim. Above them, mirrors covered the ceiling in a checkerboard pattern, reflecting back a topical view of Christine, Michael, and Jeffries.

"Mr. Lawson told me to tell you that you can see yourselves in." Katie pointed to a large set of wooden doors to the left.

"Who the hell is this guy?" Jeffries said.

"A man with intellect," Michael said.

They entered the office. Larger than the reception area, the room was filled with bookshelves on one side of the room, and to the right, floor to ceiling, were windows with a great view of the Hudson River. In the middle, Lawson sat behind a large desk. "Please sit down and make yourselves comfortable."

"Thank you Mr. Lawson. I'm detective Maloan. We spoke yesterday."

"Yes. Nice to meet you."

"This is my partner, Detective Jeffries, and this is Special Agent Michael Roberts."

The three of them sat in leather bucket chairs. Christine and Jeffries sat on either side of Michael, who sat directly across from Lawson.

Christine caught herself staring down at the desk and looked up. From a sitting position, Lawson was a big man. His thick neck held his majestic oversized head. He was a truck of a man. Her stomach turned as she looked up above Lawson. She was not accustomed to being caught off guard. Above Mr. Lawson, the eyes of a black bear peered back at her. The stuffed beast was mounted to the wall. She knew it was dead, but she could swear its eye twitched. She looked away.

"Detective, I see you're admiring my work."

"Those aren't the words I would use," said Christine.

Smiling at Michael, Mr. Lawson asked, "Do you hunt?"

"No, never have."

"That's a shame, It's so much fun."

"Not my kind of fun."

"I use different weapons, from crossbows to rifles."

"How exciting."

"Do you see the bear up there?"

Michael looked straight ahead, as Lawson pointed to the stuffed head.

"That one I killed with a hunting knife. You can't imagine how powerful that makes you feel."

"Again, not my thing."

"When you kill one of the world's most feared animals in hand to hand combat there is nothing else like it."

"Sorry Mr. Lawson, I love animals—some of them anyway."

"Ok enough with the exciting banter gentleman. Mr. Lawson we have a few questions for you." Christine said.

"Shoot."

"Mr. Lawson we understand you're quite a collector, in fact two years ago you acquired an interesting item from an auction house in Britain. An Egyptian rope."

"What about it?"

"We were wondering if you are still in possession of it," she said.

"I keep that at my cottage in the Muskokas. The last time I was there it was still in the display case in my den."

"Is this where you partake in murdering the defenseless animals?" Michael said.

Both Christine and Lawson turned to look at Michael. Christine noticed the change in Lawson. His eyes studied Michael and he leaned on his hard cherry desk. His forearm was as big as a cannon. The muscles rippled in three different places as he clenched his fist. She could see Michael's hand resting on the butt of his gun. Christine reached over and grabbed his arm. He took his hand away and it dropped to his side. Lawson's hand flew from the desk and entwined with his other hand behind his head.

"You mean hunting wild beasts, no?"

"Mr. Lawson we have a court order for you to produce that rope," Christine said.

"Why Detective I have no problem helping you with this. I will have my assistant send for it today."

"Another thing, we have a court order for a sample of the Polyethylene Glycol you distribute. We can have one of our techs collect this from your warehouse on Twelfth Street.

"That won't be necessary Detective I will have a sample sent to your office later this week."

"Sorry, our tech is out at the warehouse as we speak and she will provide a copy of the warrant to your manager. Our tech will collect the evidence," Michael said.

"You'll also need to provide us with your whereabouts for these dates." Christine handed him the search warrants for the rope, chemical, and the dates of his whereabouts during the Picasso murders."

"Am I under investigation, detective?"

"Mr. Lawson I would have thought that a man of your intelligence would understand that this is just a preliminary interview. But by all means think what you like," Michael said.

"Detective Maloan I appreciate that you are a professional. As for your Special Agent here, it's best that you get him out of my office while he's still healthy."

"Is that a threat?" Michael said.

"No, Agent Roberts. I never make threats."

They left without another word.

ELEVEN

Central Park was alive. Laughter from children mixed with the melodies of a street performer. Tim stopped to listen. Jazz floated along the air, which lured a couple walking down the path, to do the same. The three watched as if a spell was cast on them, played by the wizard of music.

The instrument, a saxophone, was strapped to a bursting belly that moved as the performer's diaphragm contracted. His white hair shifted with the rhythm. Sausage-like fingers moved swiftly along the brass instrument. Along the edge of the pond, a girl, four, maybe five, leaned over and made faces at her reflection in the calm water below. An oblivious mother gossiped about handbags sold on Canal Street. Lovers rowed along at the far end of the pond. A rhythmic sound from the splash of the oars added to the jazz melody that flowed out from the sax. Together the orchestra played a masterful symphony.

The sounds were now a lingered echo as Tim passed through the wrought iron gate of the Conservatory Gardens, a cement slab squared off a section of grass. In the middle a fountain sprayed water. The flow of trickled water filled Tim's ears as he found a seat on a wooden bench along the west side.

Tim pulled out his cell from the inside pocket of his jacket and dialed her number. On the third ring, she answered.

"Hey, lover," she said.

"Simone."

"Miss me already, huh?"

"I think it's time to step it up. Why don't you give the toy a call? I want to play another game."

"Oh yeah, what do you have in mind?"

"It's time to introduce you to my world. Would you like that, Simone?"

"I would...but can't you give me something? Tell me some of the details"

"Just set it up for Friday night. Somewhere private. And Simone, don't let me down"

He pressed the red "end" button on his Blackberry.

The fresh air inspired him. Electricity filled his veins. The moment was euphoric and all his senses were in overdrive. The park's fall colours were in full-radiance, with red and orange mixed among the green. Vivid.

At that time of the day, many people, mostly local women, visited the area. Tim hoped to find someone that would pique his interest. He had let Simone live for now and that left him dissatisfied, although, playing with Simone was something he looked forward to.

Two women walked together on the other side of the circular fountain. He heard the chatter, and noticed neither listened to the other. *Women are funny that way.*

On a bench on the other side of the path, a woman sat alone, eating her lunch. Tim watched her; he liked how she attacked her sandwich. She ripped off bite-sized-pieces and ate them. To others, she would have seemed awkward and homely. Her dark sunglasses rested on the tip of her nose. She wore a brown jacket and a white satin blouse. Her black skirt was longer than most men liked. She looked plain, he liked that. Her legs crossed at the ankles; a posture that added to the goofy demeanor.

Tim smiled.

As he walked past her, he noticed from her name tag that she worked at Macys and her name was Tina. More than likely a cashier, she didn't have the confidence to be in sales or the style to do make-up. Yes, she was perfect.

Tim followed Tina to Macys. They entered off Seventh Avenue. The air rushed at him before the door could shut behind. Tina struggled while attempting to remove her jacket. The strap of her messenger bag kept catching the button on the sleeve of her jacket. Tim took the opportunity to assist her.

"Here, let me help." Tim smiled with a warm gesture.

With a little resistance, Tina gave in. Tim slipped the caught button from the worn strap. Tina, with the grace of a drunken monkey swung off her jacket, which gave Tim just enough time to remove an item from her bag. Tim handed her back the bag, minus the wallet, that he now cupped in his hand. She turned and waved.

The men's department was quiet, which worked in his favor. He tried on ten pairs of gloves being methodical about the fit, and he compared the shades. Tim placed a glove to his nose and inhaled deeply. The warm smell of the leather filled him. His eyes closed and, with his chin tipped toward the department store lights he exhaled.

With the gloves in hand, he moved in the direction of the cashier sign. With a look of admiration, Tim smiled at the young woman behind the counter. She wore the same outfit as earlier, minus the jacket. He stepped up to pay for the gloves.

"Hi Tina."

"How do you know my name?"

Tim pointed to her nametag.

"Oh!" Pink rushed to her cheeks as she smiled.

Tim placed the wallet on the counter. Her eyes looked stunned with amazement as she took notice of the hot pink D&G knock off. Suspicion must have set in as she shot him a curious look.

"You dropped this. I tried to find you after I found it but you had vanished."

A pair of bright eyes and a sincere smile replaced the investigative glance.

"Oh my god! Thank you. I was looking for this. There's no money in it but I do need my transit card."

"It's still intact; you have my word."

"Well, thanks anyway."

Tim placed the leather gloves on the wood counter top.

"Would you like to put this on your Macy's card today? You can save ten percent off your purchase."

"No, I will pay cash if that's ok, Tina?"

"I'm sorry, sir. They make me say that you know. I think it's stupid, but it's part of my job."

"That's ok, Tina. No problem. I think you're doing a fine job."

"That'll be a hundred and forty-five then."

Tim knocked over a box, filled with credit card applications, as he handed Tina the money. Tim could swear he heard her say *shit* as she bent down to pick up the mess.

Tina stood up, frustrated from the task, and placed the box back in its rightful place.

"I'm sorry," he said.

Tina gave him his change and the Macy's bag that contained his gloves.

"Thank you for shopping at Macy's." She flashed him a forced smile.

He left the store without saying another word.

Tim spent the rest of the afternoon in Tina's apartment. Each room revealed more about her. In the refrigerator, on the top shelf stood, alone, a carton of milk with two days left before it expired. In one of the kitchen drawers Tim found cancelled cheques with rent written on the bottom. Three more post-dated ones as well.

Tina arrived at her apartment in Queens. Tim watched from behind the thick curtains as she opened the door, threw her coat on the bench, and left her keys on the bench as well. She didn't need to lock the door; it locked automatically, which he had opened using his Brockhage lock-pick. He was amused that she checked it anyway.

She slung her bag over her shoulder as she moved toward her bedroom. From this angle, Tim didn't have a clear view into the bedroom. He could hear a high-pitched squeak of the mattress springs as they compressed. Whispers of rustled clothes echoed off the concrete walls as they piled onto the wood floor.

Tina had changed into a plain-white cotton nightgown, and was now applying the last layer of mayonnaise onto her ham sandwich. She poured a large glass of milk and sat down at the small table that divided the kitchen from the living room.

Tim leered as Tina finished her dinner. She placed the empty dishes onto the stack of dirty ones that were piled high in the sink. Her gown swept the floor as she walked from the kitchen to the bedroom. Tim stalked behind her with the stealth of a spider.

She propped herself up against the headboard and turned on the TV. The Discovery Channel, another Mars Discovery Mission was on; he'd seen that one before.

Tina turned on her side, her back to the door. The TV sat on the dresser in the corner. The sound from the speakers floated to the middle of the room and stopped: the words hung above her bed frozen. He moved through the space between the door and the bed with a goal in mind. Linen-lined wicker baskets were stowed underneath. Pine posts supported the twin-sized bed.

Her bare arm was covered with fine black hairs that Tim brushed, as he passed. Time slowed, which matched his breathing. Her reaction, in comparison, was quick and immediate. Her body turned a full one hundred and eighty degrees. Her eyes opened wide. Tim almost chuckled at the sight.

He covered her mouth with the leather glove he had bought earlier. As he replaced his hand with a piece of duct tape, he wondered if she enjoyed the smell of the leather as much as he did.

With calmness, he tied her arms to the pine posts beneath. Her legs kicked back, but they were handled easily by his steady arms. He spread her legs apart, released his grip on her left leg, and then tied her right ankle to the post.

Her eyes switched from side to side as her arms pulled at the scarves.

"Tina, are you ok?" A muffled scream silenced as the low sound vibrated through the strip across her mouth.

"Tina, I need you to remain calm. Do you understand?"

Nothing.

"Tina, I don't want to hurt you." Tim revealed the eight-inch leather handled knife. Rivers of tears streamed down both sides of her face. "I have rules and I need you acknowledge them. I promise you, if you follow them you will survive."

Nothing...only tears.

"Rule number one: you won't scream."

Tina nodded her head.

"Rule number two: you will do exactly what I say."

Tina nodded her head.

"Rule number three: you will tell no one about what happens here tonight...understand?"

Tina nodded her head.

"To be sure that you fully understand the gravity of the situation I want to show you something."

Tim pulled out the post-dated-cheques he had found earlier. He placed the cheques inches away from her nose and pressed the tip of the knife into the paper. A slight indent appeared just below the name and address printed on the top left corner.

"I'm going to assume this is your father. If I find you uncooperative I may have to pay a little visit to him and introduce him to my knife."

Nothing.

"You care about him very much, don't you?"

Tina nodded.

Tim bent down, resting his lips against her ear, "Tina if you break any of the rules... I will kill him."

Tina shook her head.

"I'm going to remove the tape from your mouth. Remember, if you scream you will be breaking one of my very important rules. Do you understand?"

She nodded and he removed the tape.

"I want you to do something for me? Will you?"

A breath escaped her and with it was the soft sound of, "Yes."

"I'm going to remove your gown. Is that ok?"

Tina said nothing.

"Tina, I understand you're scared. I don't want to hurt you. I will ask you again. Can I remove your clothes?"

Tina nodded.

"Good girl."

Tim slid the knife under the collar of her nightgown and guided the blade, with precision down the middle, slicing through the material, careful not to nick her with the tip. The white cotton gown fell at her side.

Tim looked in her eyes and was thrilled to see the terror.

The panties came next.

As she lay naked in front of him, he approved. He was proud of himself. Tina was hiding something from everyone. She had large breasts, which she disguised well under her clothes. Her tummy had just a little fat, not too much that a young man would complain, but enough to make her self-conscious.

Tim was surprised that she didn't trim down below; most young women her age would have a landing strip, or would be bald. Tim liked that she was natural.

Tim was going to enjoy this—*Tina not so much*, which was of no importance to him. Tim left the room to gather the necessary items.

He returned, carrying a bowl and a towel. He placed the bowl on the bed and Tina closed her eyes. He dunked the hand towel in the bowl. The heat from the water turned his skin red. He wrung the hand towel over top of the bowl, removing the excess water. Steam rose as he placed it on her soft skin. He washed her stomach, taking care to be gentle. He continued the fluid motion over her breasts. Her nipples reacted and rose to attention. As he made another trip to the steaming water, he noticed her wide eyes on him.

"Are you ok, Tina?"

Nothing.

He placed the fresh hand towel on her pussy and cleaned her with a smooth rhythmic pace. Her hips jutted upwards, not something she intended, he was sure. After the cleaning, Tim dried her off—patting her down gently.

"Tina, I had hoped that you would have done this yourself, for me."

She looked mystified by the statement. "This was ok too. I rather enjoyed this, did you?"

Nothing.

"Tina, I need you tell me it's ok to fuck you."

Tina's scream was unexpected, but covered with his hand nonetheless.

TWELVE

Christine looked at the photos of all the victims as she sat at her desk. She noticed that with the first five victims, the killer was hesitant with the mutilation. But after the sixth, the killer changed. He built up his confidence and carved out the sexual organs with precision. She thought of Lawson and, although he had anger issues, she just couldn't picture him doing this. Jefferies entered the office. He walked in a straight line toward her, and sat on the empty chair.

"What's up?" she asked.

Christine looked at Jefferies and he was starring right through her.

"Fought with the wife this morning."

"What happened?"

"Same old shit. I work too much. We never talk anymore. What's with you women? You always need to talk."

"Hey!"

"Sorry about that. It's just fucking hard. I can't talk to her about what we do here. She wouldn't be able to stomach it."

She reached over and tapped his knee with her hand. Their eyes met, and now he was looking at her and not through her. She smiled at him and wide enough to reveal teeth. His shoulders dropped and he sat back into the chair.

"I'm fucking it up, aren't I?"

"There's still time. You can fix this. You need to open up to her. Tell her what you go through. So she understands."

"I can't do that to her. If she knew what I see here every day...I think that would ruin her."

"She's tougher than you think."

"Yeah, what about you huh? You're turning thirty-seven this year and you've never been married, no kids, no social life."

"Well, let's face it. Maybe it's not written in the books for me."

"No, you can't think that. You'll meet someone, you'll see."

Christine thought of the man she spilled coffee all over. *What was his name—Tim. Yeah that was it.* He seemed like a nice guy. It had been a while since she laughed like that. A long time.

"Have you seen Michael?" she asked.

"Nope, he didn't make it in yet today."

"Have you noticed?"

"Noticed what?"

"The way he smells. He sweats alcohol."

Christine could tell he was a drinker from the start. During the first few weeks, it was hard to get used to the stench.

Jefferies got up and turned away. "I'm going to grab a coffee. You want one?"

"Sure," she said.

Her phone rang.

"Detective Christine Maloan."

"Hi Detective, it's Tim."

"Hey, I was just thinking about you."

"Oh yeah? All good stuff, I hope."

"So what's up?"

"I just called to tell you I'm putting her down."

"Pardon? Putting who down?"

"The love of my life, my loyal servant...my suede. The dry cleaners can't get the stain out. So, I have to let her go."

"Oh shit! I'm sorry. Where did you get it? I'll get you a new one."

"Sorry, she's one of a kind. A collector's item you would say."

"Ok, how much?"

"Christine don't worry about it. It's all good."

"No, seriously. You have to let me pay for it.

"I won't have it. Really I just called to let you know," he said.

"Sorry about that. It's just fucking hard. I can't talk to her about what we do here. She wouldn't be able to stomach it."

She reached over and tapped his knee with her hand. Their eyes met, and now he was looking at her and not through her. She smiled at him and wide enough to reveal teeth. His shoulders dropped and he sat back into the chair.

"I'm fucking it up, aren't I?"

"There's still time. You can fix this. You need to open up to her. Tell her what you go through. So she understands."

"I can't do that to her. If she knew what I see here every day…I think that would ruin her."

"She's tougher than you think."

"Yeah, what about you huh? You're turning thirty-seven this year and you've never been married, no kids, no social life."

"Well, let's face it. Maybe it's not written in the books for me."

"No, you can't think that. You'll meet someone, you'll see."

Christine thought of the man she spilled coffee all over. *What was his name—Tim. Yeah that was it.* He seemed like a nice guy. It had been a while since she laughed like that. A long time.

"Have you seen Michael?" she asked.

"Nope, he didn't make it in yet today."

"Have you noticed?"

"Noticed what?"

"The way he smells. He sweats alcohol."

Christine could tell he was a drinker from the start. During the first few weeks, it was hard to get used to the stench.

Jefferies got up and turned away. "I'm going to grab a coffee. You want one?"

"Sure," she said.

Her phone rang.

"Detective Christine Maloan."

"Hi Detective, it's Tim."

"Hey, I was just thinking about you."

"Oh yeah? All good stuff, I hope."

"So what's up?"

"I just called to tell you I'm putting her down."

"Pardon? Putting who down?"

"The love of my life, my loyal servant...my suede. The dry cleaners can't get the stain out. So, I have to let her go."

"Oh shit! I'm sorry. Where did you get it? I'll get you a new one."

"Sorry, she's one of a kind. A collector's item you would say."

"Ok, how much?"

"Christine don't worry about it. It's all good."

"No, seriously. You have to let me pay for it.

"I won't have it. Really I just called to let you know," he said.

"Let me buy you dinner. It's the least I can do." It slipped out without a thought...without control of any kind. *Was she crazy?* The line was silent for what seemed to be forever, but was more like a couple seconds.

"Sure, why not?" he said.

"Do you know the Strip House?"

"Of course, great place."

"Meet me there at 8:30 Friday night."

"Friday doesn't work for me. How about Saturday?"

"That's fine. See you then and hey, sorry again about the jacket."

"Please don't worry about it. I look forward to seeing you. Bye, Christine."

With that, she hung up. Her stomach knotted up and she felt a little dizzy. Jefferies returned holding two coffees.

"Who was that?"

"A guy I dumped a latte on."

"You did what?"

"It's a long story. But it's funny I just lined up a date for Saturday night."

"Look at you. See? I told you," he said.

"Ok. So maybe I'm not completely relationship challenged," she said.

THIRTEEN

"Hey Simone. Looking good," Carl said. Her boss poked his head around the side of her grey cubical. She was wearing a top cut low enough to show the full shape of her breasts. Carl's eyes locked down on her mounds. She liked the attention.

"Thank you. Do you like my outfit? She pinched her top between her thumb and index finger and pulled to further the effect.

"Yes very nice." He stared for a moment longer and then his eyes moved from her cleavage back up to her face. "Listen, I need you to pull the Marshal Ad Mat for the "Boxing Day" flyer. We have to make some changes. Cool?"

"Cool boss," Simone said. Her hand shot to her mouse and clicked on the file.

"My office in thirty," Carl said as he disappeared from above her cubical.

"Can't wait," she said and noticed he was no longer standing there.

Tim's instructions were clear and she would do what she had to. The night they spent together at the club left her unsatisfied. He was a drug that flowed through her veins and affected her like a hit of ecstasy. She struggled with the addiction. She scrolled through her contacts until she found the name Jenny.

The phone rang twice and a smooth high-pitched voice answered back before the third ring.

"Hello?"

"Hi! It's Simone. We met the other night at the Marquee."

"Oh, hey. What's up?"

"Got any plans Friday?"

"Not yet. Why?"

"I would like to take up where we left off. Interested?" Simone said.

The line was silent as Simone waited for the response. Tim would be pissed at her if she didn't make this happen. *Fuck. Say yes.* "Well?"

"I'm thinkin. You bringing the boy?"

"Why, does it matter?"

"You bring the boy and I'm in," she said.

"Done. I'll call you tomorrow with the details. See you Friday."

The hard part was over.

She printed the Ad mat and walked down the long hallway to the color printer. Margaret looked like she was pretending to type away in a cubical across from the printer. She thought the woman could use a little more makeup and a skirt instead the grey suit she wore. The picture on her desk displayed a happy couple in their early fifties. She thought the couple looked ancient.

"Simone, can I talk to you for second?"

Simone pulled the copy from the printer and turned toward Margaret. The woman looked Simone up and down. Her lips pursed and she shook her head.

"Simone, I don't know how to say this without hurting your feelings but some of us in the office wanted to say something to you about your attire."

"Excuse me?"

"Well, the way you dress. It's well, unprofessional. You might want to tone it down a bit."

Her head swam as she decoded what the old hag just said. The comments stung for just a second. Only a second. She smiled and flashed the woman her pearly whites. Simone fondled her breasts.

"Carl doesn't seem to mind."

Margaret turned away with a look on her face as if Simone had pulled up her skirt and pissed in the woman's cubical. *Fuck you.*

Happy with the response she turned and paraded back to her desk.

She called Tim and gave him the good news. He seemed excited and elated with her—proud. She smiled.

"Can't wait," she said and noticed he was no longer standing there.

Tim's instructions were clear and she would do what she had to. The night they spent together at the club left her unsatisfied. He was a drug that flowed through her veins and affected her like a hit of ecstasy. She struggled with the addiction. She scrolled through her contacts until she found the name Jenny.

The phone rang twice and a smooth high-pitched voice answered back before the third ring.

"Hello?"

"Hi! It's Simone. We met the other night at the Marquee."

"Oh, hey. What's up?"

"Got any plans Friday?

"Not yet. Why?"

"I would like to take up where we left off. Interested?" Simone said.

The line was silent as Simone waited for the response. Tim would be pissed at her if she didn't make this happen. *Fuck. Say yes.* "Well?"

"I'm thinkin. You bringing the boy?"

"Why, does it matter?"

"You bring the boy and I'm in," she said.

"Done. I'll call you tomorrow with the details. See you Friday."

The hard part was over.

She printed the Ad mat and walked down the long hallway to the color printer. Margaret looked like she was pretending to type away in a cubical across from the printer. She thought the woman could use a little more makeup and a skirt instead the grey suit she wore. The picture on her desk displayed a happy couple in their early fifties. She thought the couple looked ancient.

"Simone, can I talk to you for second?"

Simone pulled the copy from the printer and turned toward Margaret. The woman looked Simone up and down. Her lips pursed and she shook her head.

"Simone, I don't know how to say this without hurting your feelings but some of us in the office wanted to say something to you about your attire."

"Excuse me?"

"Well, the way you dress. It's well, unprofessional. You might want to tone it down a bit."

Her head swam as she decoded what the old hag just said. The comments stung for just a second. Only a second. She smiled and flashed the woman her pearly whites. Simone fondled her breasts.

"Carl doesn't seem to mind."

Margaret turned away with a look on her face as if Simone had pulled up her skirt and pissed in the woman's cubical. *Fuck you.*

Happy with the response she turned and paraded back to her desk.

She called Tim and gave him the good news. He seemed excited and elated with her—proud. She smiled.

"Let's meet her at the Ritz and Simone, book a room."

FOURTEEN

Jeffries shuffled his feet moving the small stone on the sidewalk like a kid playing with a soccer ball as he took another drag from his cigarette. He had expected Lawson any minute and waited for him outside the precinct.

Miraculously Jeffries made it through his breakfast this morning unscathed; he avoided another battle with Teresa. She had been unusually quiet for once and, for the first time in months, he skipped the trip to the medicine cabinet for another hit of Advil.

The large black four-by-four pulled down Twenty-First Street and parked across from where Jeffries was standing. He watched as Lawson exited from the vehicle and Lawson was almost the same height as the SUV.

"Fuck you're tall," Jeffries called out to Lawson.

"Thanks Detective."

"No, thank you for coming in."

"It's my pleasure."

The interview room was bright and the white table glared from the lights overhead. Michael entered the room and Christine followed behind them. The agent sat in front of Lawson and threw down a manila file folder between them on the table. Lawson's eyes never moved to the file. Instead, they trained directly on Michael.

"Well, Mr. Lawson. We all appreciate you blessing us with your presence."

"You know something, Agent? For someone with your eating habits, I would be more concerned with your life expectancy than trying to be witty. Believe me. I'm not amused. What do you want?"

Jeffries reviewed the names of all the Picasso victims. After he finished announcing the third name, and the latest victim found at St. Patrick's, he asked Lawson if he knew any of them.

"Why is this of any relevance?"

"Just answer the question, Lawson," Michael said.

"Agent Roberts I know you think you're smart. And you may have even attended college. But, you obviously you have no people skills. To answer your questions detective Jeffries, no I don't."

Michael opened the file and placed pictures of all four victims in front of Lawson. The images of the bodies seemed to transfix him. Lawson picked up the image of the woman on the tower. He looked it over and placed it back down on the table.

"Nice picture." He smiled.

"You find something funny Lawson? Because I don't. By the way, can you explain to me how the chemical you distribute matched the same chemical we found on all these victims?" Michael asked.

Jeffries watched as Lawson's smile widened.

"How would I know? I sell the stuff to hundreds of customers across the country."

"We'll need those customer logs," Christine said.

"Yeah but that wouldn't explain the ropes. Now would it. It's all too coincidental. Lawson, I don't think your muscles are going to dig you out of this one!" Michael said.

"You're admiring my pipes Michael. Is that because deep down inside, you're attracted to me. Are you one of those types?" Lawson asked.

"Lawson, we haven't received the ropes, any reason for the delay?" Christine asked.

Jeffries didn't like the way Michael and Lawson were looking at each other. There was something in their eyes, Jeffries had seen, too many times on the job.

"Well? Answer the detective." Michael said.

"Sorry if I'm not working within your time lines. My assistant is the one making the arrangements. You will have it soon."

"When? Give me a date," Michael said.

"Listen, I'm trying to be courteous. As we all know, the rope is at my cottage in Canada and that warrant isn't worth the paper it's printed on. So, if you're not happy with the timing, contact the Canadian authorities and follow the proper procedures. Is that all? If so, I have a meeting to attend."

"What's your hurry? Are you feeling uncomfortable?" Michael said.

"Mr. Lawson we appreciate your assistance and we're trying to eliminate you as a suspect," Christine said.

"That's just not good enough for me. By the sounds of it you think of yourself as a man that gets things done and you can't give us something as simple as a tracking number for the package containing the ropes," Michael said.

"Listen to me, you life-size Twinkie. Unless you are arresting me, right now. Which we all know, there isn't enough on me to do, I will be leaving." Lawson rose from the metal chair and placed his pole-sized arms on the desk towering over Michael. "Would you like to go hunting Agent Roberts?"

"That's the second time he's threatened me. I hope you detectives heard that."

"Are you always this paranoid Agent," Lawson said.

Lawson moved from behind the desk and saluted Christine. She opened the door and escorted him out.

"What's wrong with you Michael?" Jeffries said.

"What?"

"Why do you need to go after him like that? You know we don't have enough on him yet. We could have used a little more time with him today. Maybe he would've let something slip. I thought they taught that up in Quantico." Jeffries said.

He left Roberts alone in the room and followed Christine out into the office. She was walking Lawson out of the precinct when he caught up to her.

"Hey Lawson," Jeffries said and Lawson turned toward him. "Listen, sorry about that back there. You know the FBI type. Anyway, we still need your help. If you could send us that customer log, we could really use it. The ropes too. We just want to eliminate you as a suspect. The last thing we want to do is waste time on you. We need to catch this maniac."

"You see, Christine, with a little butter everything tastes better," Lawson said.

"Detective, because you asked so nicely I will agree to your request about the customer log. No warrant needed. Regarding the rope, I'll personally look into it today," Lawson said.

As Lawson drove away, Christine smacked Jeffries in the shoulder.

"What was that all about?" she asked.

"You know we don't have enough to pin anything on Lawson. As he said, he just distributes the stuff. Who knows how many people have access to the wax?"

"Then how do you explain the ropes? Let's face it, the guy's hiding something. I know it."

"Yeah, well, chasing him away isn't going to help. I'd rather keep him involved in the investigation."

Christine nodded. "Listen, I have to visit my parents tonight. Dinner. Can you cover for me?"

"No problem."

FIFTEEN

Tim called, using his Bluetooth-hands-free, from the car to
let Simone know he was downstairs.

The news about the Asian moved along his plan to school Simone in the craft. *His craft.* Asking him to come with her to her sister's for drinks tonight was a bonus and he took this opportunity to test Simone. People will do almost anything under the right circumstances. He knew this.

Simone rushed to the car. She tapped hard on the driver's side window and ran around to the passenger door like a boy that just lost his virginity and was up for another round in the sac.

Tim let her open the door herself and she swung in, kissing him hard on the lips, leaving behind the taste of orange lip-gloss.

During the ride, the gossip flowed. Simone's dam of secrecy burst open and she revealed her sister's dirty laundry. Samantha and Doug had been married for ten years. No kids. No pets. Both focused on their careers; Samantha worked in sales for a high-end art gallery and Doug worked as a Stock Broker on Wall Street. He thought her description of Doug was amusing—*bald geek.*

The lights from the buildings flashed across the windshield as Tim calculated his next comment.

"Do you think you're hot?" he asked. He took his eyes off of the road long enough to notice Simone's reaction to the question. Her recent glow of confidence dulled for a second.

"Of course. Don't you?"

"How hot?" he asked.

"Sizzling!"

The glow was back and brighter than the LED signs that littered Broadway.

"Doug...you think you could get him off?"

"What?" she asked with a stunned look in her eyes.

"You can't touch him."

"What do you mean?"

"Make him cum without taking it out of his pants. Can you do it?"

"I don't know. Why?"

"Sizzling huh?" He shifted down and swerved to the right to pass the slow moving car in front him. When he was safe and back in the lane, he looked over at Simone. He wasn't smiling.

"I could do it!" she said.

"Good. I'll leave it up to you on how you do it. I think that by the sounds of it Doug hasn't had much action in a while. It should be no problem."

"I know."

"Then it's settled. It will be fun. Trust me."

They arrived at Samantha's at eight. Samantha greeted them at the door. She was stunning. Her straight blonde hair hung down past her shoulders. The highlights blended in and it was obvious to Tim that the sisters spent a fortune styling their hair. Other than that, he found no other similarities. The neckline of her red dress was short enough to reveal cleavage but covered enough not to make her look like a slut. Samantha was classy—sophisticated.

Doug trailed behind her. Tim wasn't surprised; Doug was as Simone described—average. Actually everything about Doug was average, from his lack of hair to his clothes especially his face. He was not bad looking but he wasn't good-looking either. If you passed him in the street, you would forget him within seconds. Tim couldn't understand why Samantha married the man.

"Come on in, guys." Samantha said.

Tim handed Samantha a bottle of wine that he had brought from his collection.

"Would you like something to drink Tim?" Doug asked.

"Sure."

"What can I get you?"

"If you have Crown, I'll take it over ice with a splash of Diet Coke. If not, a beer will do."

"Tim, no problem. My liquor cabinet's fully stocked. Follow me," Doug said.

Tim followed Doug into the den.

Doug poured two drinks, handing one to Tim.

"So Samantha tells me that you and Simone just met."

"Yes, it was luck; some would call it fate."

"Yeah, we love Simone," Doug said.

"She's a very special woman."

"You like the Rangers, Tim?"

Tim turned his attention to the flat screen on the wall. The Rangers game was on.

"Nice choice Tim. Mondovi is one of my favorites. Thanks for bringing it," Samantha said as she walked into the room.

Simone followed her sister into the den with a wine glass in her hand. Doug was sitting in the lounger and Samantha sat across from him on the sofa. The Rangers were behind Toronto 2-1 and Doug cursed as Nick Antropov fired a puck into the net. Tim sat between Samantha and Simone. "You like living downtown?" Tim asked.

Doug's eyes lifted off the TV just enough to join in on the conversation and reply to Tim's question. "I love it."

"Doug wouldn't care where we lived as long as he had a TV and a hockey game to watch," Samantha said.

"Don't be so hard on him, Sis. All guys love sports."

Simone undid her top three buttons and with the right angle, there was a clear view of her tit. She positioned herself toward Doug and smiled. Tim watched as Doug caught a full glimpse. His eyes widened; glued to her chest. Simone was a good girl she followed his directions with the skill of a well-trained dog.

She uncrossed her legs; her skirt opened about four inches, traveled up her thighs, and Doug's eyes popped. The game could have been 4-1 for the Rangers, but right now, Tim could tell that was the last thing on Doug's mind.

"Hey Sam, why don't you give Tim a tour?" Simone said.

Doug said nothing. He was lost in the deep confines of Simone's crotch.

"Ok! Anything's better than watching hockey."

Samantha grabbed Tim by the hand and escorted him out of the den.

"Well, you've seen the kitchen... Follow me."

Tim walked hand-in-hand with Samantha down the hallway. She stopped to show him pictures that hung on the wall. The wedding photos and Samantha's family portrait. The girls' mother was just as beautiful as the two sisters were—Samantha, of course, the prettier of the two.

They climbed the back staircase to the second floor. Tim wondered how Doug was handling himself. Or Simone for that matter.

The second floor landing opened up to a long hallway that covered the length of the condominium. The Berber covered floor made his feet warm.

"And this is our second floor suite, fully equipped with three bedrooms; and the back room has an eight-person hot tub."

"You're kidding me?" he said.

"Yep, Doug had it installed last Christmas. A present for me. He hasn't gone in it yet."

"That's a shame. I bet you would look hot topless in there."

Perfect timing. The comment hit home and she gulped.

She looked at him with a shy expression as if to say... *Who me? I wouldn't do that.*

He knew she would.

He was great at understanding what made woman tick. It would just take some convincing, and a little insight from Simone didn't hurt.

"Show me," he said.

She looked back at him with a strange expression. With a *"What are you asking?"* kind of look.

"The hot tub?" she said.

"If you want to... you're giving the tour."

"Ok."

She pulled him along to the far end of the hall. It opened up to a large room. Ceramic tiles covered the floor and ended at the cedar stairs that led up the edge of the tub. Trickling water ran down a faux waterfall made of slate that hung from the wall behind the hot tub.

"It's a little much, huh?" she said.

"I think it's fantastic. I bet the waterfall was your idea."

He knew the answer to that comment—information given to him by Simone during the ride over—he also knew that Samantha and Doug hadn't had sex in eight months. And about their recent fight. Something about how late Doug works. By now, Doug must be rock hard and wanting to slobber all over Simone. She was that good, but she also followed the rules. His rules.

"Want to go for dip?" he asked.

"What? No way, you're joking!"

"The water looks hot."

She looked at him with an odd expression. He softened his eyes and he smiled with a smile that could relax a drug addict on meth. She looked again and this time she tilted her head off to one side. She squinted, and her lips straightened.

"Samantha, I'm kidding."

"I knew you were. Like we would just jump into the hot tub. I just met you, for God sakes."

If Tim knew Simone, and he did, then Doug would be so lost in attraction right now not even the Wizard of Oz could send him home.

Samantha dragged Tim down the hallway, again hand-in-hand, and the moment of tension seemed to pass. Life in the house of Samantha had fallen back into its perfect little slot. He smiled all the way down the stairs.

"Wait." He pulled on her arm before they entered the room. She was close to him. Close enough that he could make out tiny flecks in her iris. Above her top lip, a mist of sweat. She held her breath and her chest met his.

"What?" she whispered.

"What do you think they're doing in there?"

"What do you mean? Simone? Doug? Doing what?"

He moved back and she turned and walked into the room. Tim followed behind her. Simone's shirt was buttoned to the top, her legs were crossed, and she sat in the same seat as before. The game was in the last five minutes of the third period, Toronto was up 5-4, and there was a wet spot on Doug's pants.

"Simone baby, we have to get going."

Up she sprung like a Jack Russell after seeing its own reflection in a mirror. *Good dog.*

SIXTEEN

Lawson watched through the window of his Suburban, which fit in among the executive Limos that traveled the Manhattan streets driving suits to meetings, dinner, and strip clubs. It was a perfect vehicle for his hobby.

Beethoven's "Symphony Number Seven" played through the SUV's speaker system. It was one of his favorites and he played it on every hunt. Tonight would be no different and it was going to be exquisite.

The door of the bar opened with large arcing swing as Michael stumbled out of the bar. The detective was moving in a slow methodical pattern. He braced himself on the brick wall and slouched over. Hot steam rose from the ground.

Michael moved with more of a goal in mind leaving behind the result of one too many drinks. Lawson was not impressed. It was going to be too easy.

Michael's car pulled out onto the street. The front-end swiped the bumper of a Honda Accord. The alarm sounded and the lights flashed as he drove past the parked car.

Lawson followed him onto Third Avenue. The car weaved between lines of yellow cabs. A few honked while others swerved to avoid a collision. People walking on the sidewalks turned their heads. Lawson was sure that Michael was completely unaware of the havoc he was causing.

Ten Minutes later, Lawson followed Michael's car in to the parking lot. The vehicle rolled down the slope and the brake lights flashed. The garage door began its ascend. Lawson slipped in before the door could shut and the automatic sensor stopped the door from slamming down on the hood of the SUV and rose for the second time.

A soft hum coming from the engine echoed off the concrete slabs. The antenna slapped at the overhead pipes as he followed Michael's car down the far wing of the lot. He could see the brakes pump as Michael pulled into the space. He lowered the windows of the SUV and listened closely. Other than the running engine, there were no other sounds: no footsteps and no other cars. Only the soft hum of the Suburban.

They were alone.

Lawson rolled the SUV in a straight line and stopped behind Michael's Car. The detective was half way out of the door as Lawson approached without concealing his footsteps.

"Hi, Michael."

"Huh?"

Now the pain. No amount of alcohol would numb the thousand volts of electricity that Lawson shot through Michael's body; that Lawson was sure of. The second zap had him flipping like a wet carp on a sandy beach desperate for fresh water.

SEVENTEEN

Rockefeller Square was lit up with Christmas lights and couples skated there, holding hands. The image was serene. He moved among the tourists, scanning the women and making mental notes. Christmas was one holiday that held different memories for Tim. The kind that leave scars. He moved down 50th Street with thoughts of Christmas, and he wondered why so many enjoyed the season. For him, it was a day to remember. Some celebrated the birth of their savior, while he mourned the loss of his childhood.

***

The house was decorated. A new tree replaced the ugly white one and this time it was decked out in silver ornaments; not the blue kind that haunt his dreams. Tinsel hung from every branch. Berta was sent away for the holidays and it was just Tim and his *Mother* this Christmas.

On Christmas day Ann gave him presents, not money. Tim opened box after box—nice clothes, a CD player, and a gold chain.

Tim, at the time, didn't know what to make of it. But he accepted the change even though it felt foreign.

The following days were unlike any others Tim had spent with Ann. She gave him full run of the house and he was allowed to eat anything from the cabinets or the refrigerator. All he wanted.

On New Year's Eve, Ann told him that he could watch a movie and order a pizza. She left him money. On her way out, she turned to him. "You're thirteen this year Tim. You're a man now, and you should be treated like a man. You understand?"

Tim nodded. He didn't feel like a man. There was peach fuzz under his arms but nothing on his balls yet.

"And men are allowed to drink."

"Huh?"

"That's right Tim. I left some beer in the fridge. Drink a few, but not all of them. Ok."

"Really? Um, ok then. Thanks Ann."

"Tim, I'm going to be late, but I'll be back by midnight, make sure you're up."

She left.

After the third beer, he started to feel weird. He laughed at parts of the movie that were just not that funny.

He was watching The Shining on the Movie channel and the frightening scenes were not funny at all but he was amused anyway. It didn't matter. He laughed and laughed. The night moved in slow motion after the fourth beer. He walked from room to room seeing things for the first time through a different set of eyes. They were a little more inquisitive and little less inhibited. He ruffled through drawers that were off limits, and opened closet doors that should have been closed. *Damn, if she found him.*

He watched the ball drop in Times Square from the comfort of his sofa. The TV was usually off limits, but she had been so casual. The whole thing was confusing.

He gulped down the last swallow from the brown bottle as people celebrated the New Year on television. Five beer bottles lined the table and it was hard for him to keep them all in focus. The room began to spin little by little and then faster. On odd sensation rushed inside. He ran from the sofa to the downstairs bathroom. He vomited and filled the cold water below. The bowl filled with a kaleidoscope of colors.

With his belly empty and feeling unstable, he scaled the stairs to his room. With each step forward, he had to hold the railing to stop himself from falling backward.

Tim woke from the sound of the laughter. He raised his head; he still felt heavy but at least the room had stopped spinning. He opened his bedroom door and laughter echoed up from the floor below. He reached the top of the second floor landing and he could see them. They were both moving toward the bottom of the staircase, swaying, spilling red wine, and kissing. Their hands were touching places on each other and it made him feel dirty. It was gross. They were both women and what they were doing didn't feel right to him.

Tim stumbled. His back hit the wall. Tim could still hear them. Ann was calling his name. Then the other woman was calling out to him. The voices got louder as they climbed the stairs. He could hear them clearer now. They were giggling and calling out to him. He crept to the door of his room and braced himself against the frame. He closed the door behind him as he laboured to his bed.

Then it was quiet. They were outside his door. He could hear the whispers seeping in underneath. The door opened.

Mother walked in first.

She was still wearing her dress from the party and it was loose at the front. The strings that were once tied in a bow, hung down and swayed as she walked toward him. The embarrassment brought redness to his cheeks. Her right breast slipped in and out of the opening of her dress. It was like watching the aftermath of a car accident. He couldn't pull his eyes away.

In the doorway, her friend stood, leaning against the frame. She was also in a dress. Her red hair flowed down past her shoulders. She looked younger than his mother did. She was tall. There was something about her eyes;

they were glazed over and full of desperation. She was looking straight at him. The tip of her tongue slipped between her lips and made a full rotation around her mouth.

His mother reeked. It was strong. It seeped from her pores. The aroma of alcohol filled the room. His mind moved in and out of focus as his mother crossed the room and sat on the edge of his bed. She placed her hand on his leg.

"Tim, you've gotten so big."

She waved her friend over. She came. The friend was on the bed—and on him! The weight of her hips pushed hard into him. He said nothing because he couldn't. His voice sealed within.

"Tim, my friend needs your help. She is going to need your full cooperation, do you understand?"

Tim said nothing.

"Tim, I need you to say it's ok. You would do anything for your mother, wouldn't you?" Ann asked.

His mind was splashing in the waves of puzzlement, and the current was strong. He struggled for understanding.

He nodded.

"Good."

Ann removed the woman's dress, slipping the strap over her head. The dress fell off her shoulders down to her waist. He had a full frontal view of the woman's body, her dark skin, and her bare breasts. The way her nipples pointed out, like the girls in the magazines. And he was captivated. He noticed a small puff of black hair that covered the top of her vagina. He knew what a vagina was, and at thirteen, he knew all the correct words for the anatomy. He also knew what an erection was and he had one.

He watched as the friend touched Ann's breast. They looked at each other with hunger. He could feel himself slipping and his mind was cloudy.

Tim's eyes met Ann's. She looked back at him and there was no love. There was nothing.

Tim felt his pants slip down passed his knees. The friend grabbed his penis. He felt her hand around him. It was wet and slick. She pushed herself on him. It felt weird and electric at the same time. She moved in a rhythmic motion. Not up and down but more rocking. His groin was wet and he felt warm fluid drip down his leg.

Ann put her mouth on the woman's breast and cupped the other in her hand. She pinched her and the woman let out a moan. The friend pushed down hard on him. His hips hurt, his legs hurt, his mind hurt. Then it came like a warm river; he was soaked, the bed was soaked, and as quick as it started, it ended.

The door closed before he opened his eyes. He felt messy and sticky. His eyes were blank and distant.

Sleep settled in along with the darkness, and he slept.

The next day Ann sent him back to boarding school and Tim didn't return until his eighteenth birthday.

***

Tim arrived at the front revolving doors. He didn't remember walking the seven blocks between Rockefeller Centre and the Ritz. He moved through the doors and looked to the left into the lounge. He could see Simone sitting in the back corner, and the anorexic goddess was tucked in beside her. He scanned the rest of the lounge. It was packed. *Perfect.*

"Hey, I'm Jenny," she said as she extended a hand to Tim.

He kissed it. "Tim, it's my pleasure."

"Hey, you!" Simone said.

"What are you girls drinking?" Tim asked.

"Something strong. Martini's," Simone said.

Simone waved to the waiter. He arrived and took their orders. By the empty glasses, Tim knew they were on their third round. He thought of the warm whisky that would soon be on his lips and his mouth watered.

The lounge was busy with suits and skirts. The waiter moved through the crowd and was back with their drinks faster than Tim expected. *He wants a good tip.*

"I like how you dance," he said.

"Thanks, are we going to hit a club later?" Jenny asked.

"I was thinking we could skip the foreplay and go somewhere a little more private. Is that cool with you?" Tim said.

"Cool with me. I take it you have a room or something?"

"Something like that. No rush though. Let's have a couple of drinks first."

"You trying to get me drunk? Cause if so, there's no need," she said.

He raised his glass and they all toasted.

"Here's to a fun night."

EIGHTEEN

Michael woke up in a dark concrete room. His back hurt and his head throbbed. Breathing alone caused shooting pains. The floor was cold. A grey steel door in front of him felt solid. There was no window in it, no handle for that matter. He got up, stumbling as he did so.

Off balance, he fell into the door. His whole body shook and his teeth slammed together. He tried to push open the door but it wouldn't budge. He slammed his fist against it "Hey! Hey, you mother fucker! Let me out of here!"

Another sharp pain shot behind his eyes. He stopped. He slumped back and slid down the wall. On his ass with his feet spread out, he scanned the room. It was dark, hard to make out the back of the room, and anyone could be lurking in the shadows. He reacted by shooting his hand to his holster. No gun.

It was just so damn dark back there. It was unnerving, not knowing. He pushed up, using the wall for support, and sidled his way down the wall and into the darkness. His arm was flat to the wall and his fingers reached timidly an inch at a time. He jammed his fingers as he reached the far wall and he squeezed them into a fist until the pain subsided. From what he could tell, the room was small.

He heard the lock click. The hair on the back of his neck rose and he held his breath. The door opened a crack. Without the gun, he felt mortal. He waited in silence for what he thought was two minutes.

Nothing.

On the tips of his toes, he traveled back to the door. Ten steps and he felt the hard steel. He pushed it open with just enough room for his head to slide through. He looked in both directions. No sign of anyone. The short hallway led to a door on the left. On the right was a dead end. Overhead a series of ballasts held long florescent tubes that lit up the hallway. He crept toward the door.

It opened up to a massive warehouse; parallel catwalks lined either side of the wall and hung about ten feet from the roof. Down to the middle of the warehouse, stacked crates blocked off a good portion of the floor. Three pathways, lined with yellow paint traced out the space between the crates and cement poles jutted up from the floor on each corner. *What is this place?*

To the left light glowed through an office window. He could see that the door was open but he had no idea if

Lawson was waiting in there. He took a quick look through the window. The room was empty. He dashed in and shut the door behind him.

The office back wall was clean white concrete, no pictures or shelves; a filing cabinet leaned up against the far wall and directly behind the window sat a plain steel desk. *A phone.* He picked up the receiver and dialed 911—no ring tone. *Fuck.* He searched the drawers in the desk.

Nothing.

Michael jumped as the phone screamed out. He picked up the plastic receiver.

"Hello, hello? Please help me. I'm a Federal Agent!"

"Michael, God helps those who help themselves," Lawson said.

"Lawson!" Michael spat back.

"Calm down, Michael, you need to think," Lawson said.

"What do you want?"

"In time Michael, in due time. First, you need to understand why you're here."

"Understand what? That you're fucking lunatic!"

"Michael...Michael...Michael. You have no tact."

"Fuck you, Lawson. I'm done playing your game. I'm going to walk right out of here and you're not going to stop me."

"Michael now that's the spirit. In fact, in the filing cabinet behind you you'll find a knife. The exit's down at the far end of the warehouse. Do you see the red light to the right?"

Michael said nothing but he could see the red light in the distance.

"That's your exit Michael. Make it there and you're home free. Don't...well I think you might have a different outcome."

The line went dead silent.

Michael pulled open the drawers one by one: empty, empty, empty. *Shit.*

The bottom drawer contained the knife. He pulled out the large Bowie. It felt heavy in his hand. The long blade gleamed from the office lights. He could see his refection in the blade. His hair was dark and full of sweat. His face was white; there was touch green as well.

With a deep breath, he opened the door and pushed out. He stuck out his chest and pulled his shoulders back. *Who was he kidding?* He was out of shape, his lungs hurt from the years of tobacco abuse, and Lawson was the size of Mack truck on steroids. The knife was his only chance—if he could just get close enough.

Michael made his descent down the row of crates. He was cautious; he stopped after a few steps and listened for movement. All he could hear was his heart pounding in his chest.

Farther down, the yellow paint turned on a right angle and a fence sectioned off the back half of the warehouse. He passed a forklift. A long red cable, fit with a plastic clamp, ran to a large electrical box that hummed on the floor and it seemed to be re-charging the forklift's battery. He tiptoed through the section of shelving that ran down the last stretch of the back half of the warehouse.

Then he heard it. It was a booming sound; like wood smacking into a hollow pipe. It had the sound of a bass drum thumping out decibels that should implode an eardrum. He jumped out of his shoes. His chest hurt and his stomach knotted up. There were two directions he could go, straight down the left side and against the far wall, or move down along the fence. He counted eight rows of shelving. Eight pathways all lead to his freedom; only Lawson was waiting in one of them.

He took the route along the fence. He paused at each pathway peeking around. He made it to the last row with no sign of Lawson.

The knife added some comfort. He noticed he was gripping the handle so tight that white spots formed on his knuckles. As he looked around the corner, he saw the red glow of the exit sign. It was mocking him. Waving to him. *Come on you can do it. It's only fifty feet or so.* He was so close. He was almost out. Fifty-feet to freedom. He made a run for it.

He felt his fat jiggling around his waist as his legs pumped. A sharp odor seeped out from his pores and he caught a whiff of his own stench. The opening was now only a few feet away. He breeched it and a flash of light blinded him. His eyes stung as he was washed in a sea of light. He blinked repeatedly and his eyes adjusted enough that he could make out a shape in front of him.

"Well Michael...you almost made it."

Lawson stood between the door and his freedom. He scanned both directions. The back wall had two huge receiving doors with the same concrete posts on either side. He took in a deep breath and his lungs burned. There was no other way out but through Lawson. He made his move. Gripping the knife's handle, he ran full speed at Lawson. "Fuck you!"

It was over fast. He felt the crushing pain of Lawson's grip on his wrist. The blood flow stopped and his hand turned white. He tried to swing with his free arm, but the pain from his wrist buckled him. Then he heard the pop in his wrist and darkness flashed behind his eyes and small white dots faded into the black. The knife dropped to the floor. Michael looked up just in time to see the fist coming. His jaw exploded. It felt like his head was coming of his body. His mouth filled with blood and darkness fell over him like a blanket of snow.

Dark.

Michael opened his eyes and he could see the floor beneath him. Rusty screws held the drain in place in the floor. He pulled on his arms but they were cuffed behind his back. He could feel the cold steel around his wrists. The one that had held the knife now throbbed. He tried moving his lower jaw but there was no controlling it. It felt loose. With his tongue, he felt around the back of his teeth and the tip of his tongue slipped into the empty space where his molar used to be. Pain shot through his cheekbone and stopped the discovery.

He looked up again and could see the tips of his feet sticking out over his gut.

"I was wondering if you were ever going to wake up. I thought I killed you. Your glass jaw shattered and I hardly even put my back into it."

Michael didn't respond. He just swung from his ankles.

"Do you want to know something?" Lawson said.

Michael tried to respond but his jaw wouldn't receive the messages sent from his brain. All he got out was muffled grunt.

"If you were smart. If you were professional like the other detectives, you would not be in the situation you're in right now. Pathetic. A disgrace to society—and I think the only right thing to do—is to put you down."

Lawson slipped around in front of him. He was holding the knife. *No. No Don't. Stop.* The blade disappeared into his gut. Warm fluid rushed down his face as he hung by his ankles. The blood flowed into his nostrils and a coppery smell filled his senses. All the light drifted from him—darkness, numbness, then nothing but the deepest of sleeps.

NINETEEN

Jenny was lying on the bed in her bra and panties, her black hair pulled out of the bun and hanging down her shoulders. The bed had a brown headboard and the bedspread was plush with gold flower arrangements woven into the fabric. Tim turned up the volume on the stereo as Joss Stone sang. Her husky voice belted out "Got a right to be wrong." *Nice touch.*

He waved over both Simone and Jenny. They met in the middle of the room and Simone pulled Jenny into her. Simone's bare breasts pressed up against Jenny's bra and they kissed swaying to the music.

"Now, that's what I'm talking about," he said.

"Oh, you like that Tim?" Jenny said.

She had no idea what he liked, but she would soon find out.

He rose from the chair and ran a finger along Jenny's shoulders. Slid his hand down her back and undid her bra, walked past the two women and left the bedroom.

"Hey get back here you," Jenny said.

He pulled a bag out of the hall closet. The leather strap squeaked as he carried it to the bedroom. Simone was lying on top of Jenny on the bed. She pinned her down in a form of aggression. She bit Jenny, and Jenny giggled.

Tim moved around to the side of the bed and placed the bag down on the floor. He pulled out four scarves and handed one to Simone.

"We're going to tie you up. Is that cool?" he asked.

"Oh yeah. You guys are freaky, I like it," she said.

Tim tied her left arm while Simone tied the right. Simone made eye contact with him and her eyes revealed a story—one he knew too well.

The woman's arms and legs were tied with the same style of silk scarves that he has used many times before this night and would soon use on Christine.

Simone snaked down Jenny's stomach kissing it as she did so. Tim climbed to the top of the bed and in one smooth motion, slipped the gag in Jenny's mouth, and clipped the strap in place.

Jenny's eyes stilled. Her body stiffened but she didn't resist. Tim reached down into the bag pulled out the device and handed it to Simone, which she gladly accepted.

"I have to pee first," Simone said, and she left the room holding the strap and the rubber penis dangling below.

Tim stretched out on the bed beside Jenny. Her dark eyes looked back at him as he guided his hand millimeters from the skin on her stomach and drew in circles. She pulled on the scarves as he teased her. The comforter bunched up underneath as she squirmed.

"You like that?"

She nodded.

"You want more?"

She nodded.

He moved down her stomach and traced lines just a hair's distance from her skin. Her eyes begged for his touch. He didn't. He could hear Simone in the washroom and the sounds of her piss streaming into the cold water in the toilet bowl.

"Jenny."

She looked at him.

"I'm going to stab you twelve times," he said.

She stilled as the words hit home. She looked at him and he could tell that she was questioning his comment. What she saw in his eyes must have convinced her because immediately her body flailed about and she pulled at the scarves.

Simone walked out of the bathroom and she looked hilarious wearing the strap-on.

"What's with her?" she said.

"Nothing. She's ready for you," he said as he pointed to Jenny.

Simone was deep inside her and Jenny was reeling back. Her gagged mouth muffled the screams that seeped through. The gag was wet and shone Turkey red. He stepped behind Simone and slid the tip of the knife along her spine and she arched her back in response. He guided the knife down her to her ass that was wet with sweat. He dropped the tip down and pricked Jenny's thigh.

She screamed out; no one would hear. He moved in behind Simone and her ass bucked into him as she pushed in and out. Her triceps flexed as she held Jenny down. Tim was looking over Simone's shoulder and Jenny's eyes were wide open. Her hips flailed back as she tried to break free of Simone's grasp.

Tim exchanged the knife from his hand to hers and, clasping his hand over Simone's, he guided the knife down into Jenny's stomach. The blade caused a sucking sound as he pulled it back out and the blood cast off coated the front of Simone's chest. He heard the vacuum-sucking noises eleven more times.

TWENTY

The Strip House was crammed at the front entrance. Christine pushed between two men in suits, both laughing.

"Excuse me, gentlemen."

The one turned toward Christine and smiled, waving her through. She stepped between the talkers and approached the host. The front of the strip house was tight. It was hot.

"Hi. Do you have a reservation?"

"Yes, Maloan for two."

"Ok. Got it, for 8:30. Were running a little late tonight. It will be about ten minutes. Your table should be ready by eight-forty. Please have a drink at the bar and the coat check is on the right."

"Ok, thank you."

Christine stepped through the talkers again and pushed her way back through the entrance and out to the street. She looked at her Timex. It read 8:20. She looked up and down Twelfth Street. Parked cars lined both sides and it was as tight as an asthmatic's lungs during an attack. She always wondered what tourists must think while trying to navigate through the congested streets of Manhattan. It was crazy tough.

She noticed Tim as he walked down the sidewalk. He was wearing a different jacket. It was black with straight lines faintly visible on the sleeves. He was taller than she remembered and looked like he had a fresh haircut.

"Hey," he said

"Hey."

"You look fantastic," he said.

"Thanks."

"It's nice to see you out of your cop clothes."

"Hey, watch it. I have my gun underneath this dress."

He smiled. They both smiled.

"New jacket?"

"Actually, an old one, but it just made the top of my favorite's list."

She laughed. *He's funny.*

"Sorry again, Tim."

"Really no problem. I always welcome change. Plus, you're buying me dinner. All's good."

"Shall we eat?" She said.

The restaurant was chic and seductive. Crushed red velvet covered the room and pictures of half-naked women hung along the walls. The lighting was dim, which created an exotic atmosphere. The bar was jammed and lined with patrons most of whom were drinking. Liquor bottles sat on revolving posts behind the bartender and he was busy filling Martini glasses. Christine made eye contact with the bartender.

"What can I get you?" he said.

"I'll have a Crown and Diet...Tim?"

"I'll have the same," he said. "So you're a Crown drinker."

She smiled back at him and laid her purse on the bar. "It does the job."

Christine pulled the glass up to her mouth and took a long swallow. The warm liquid coated the back of her throat and lit a fire in her stomach. The effect of the whisky was quick and numbed the stress. She watched Tim do the same. She lowered her glass as the hostess showed up to escort them to their table.

They were given a booth on the left and Tim sat beside her. Before the hostess took her first stride away, the waiter appeared. He was sporting a plain white dress shirt and a black tie that hung loose at the neck. He had a thick white napkin folded over his right forearm and he presented the wine list to Tim. The waiter looked serious, as if he had something important to say. He was a black man with short-cropped hair. Young but had a look of hardness to him. His voice was smooth and rhythmic.

"Good evening folks. Do you mind if I tell you about our fantastic wine list?"

"Please," Tim said and took the list.

He made few grunts. She observed Tim place the wine list aside and he stared intently at the anxious young waiter.

"If you like red cabs we have a beautiful Joseph Phelps, 'Bacchus'. The wine is powerful, broodingly tannic. If you're ordering red meat, it will bring forth all the spices. It will make the meat taste like fireworks are exploding in your mouth.

"How much?" Christine said.

"Two-forty."

"We'll take it," Tim said.

She gulped and shot Tim a surprised look as if to say *Are you serious?*

"I'll pick up the wine. You can you can take care of the meal. Cool?"

The waiter smiled revealing his crooked whites, "Perfect." He handed out the menus—first to Christine, then to Tim, and left as fast as he appeared.

"Expensive tastes, I see."

"Why not? It's not every day a cop buys me dinner."

She laughed.

"So tell me, Christine."

"Tell you what?"

"What made you decide to become a cop in the first place?"

"Well, that's a funny story. A total stereotype."

"Go on."

"Well, my dad was a cop. I grew up around cops my whole life. I looked up to my dad and his friends. They were like celebrities to me. Stupid, huh?"

"No, not at all."

"After I graduated from college I went straight to the academy and, well, here I am."

"Let me guess, you don't regret it."

"Nope. Not one bit. It took me a long time to move up to detective and now I think I'm doing something I can be proud of. I help the community. I put the bad guys away."

The waiter arrived with the bottle and displayed the label so that Tim could read it. She watched as he nodded to the waiter. Tim smiled at her as the waiter removed the cork and his smile made her think of chocolate. It was sweet and warm. She melted inside from his deep dimples. She liked men who looked rough but clean cut at the same time. If they had straight white teeth, well that was her hot button and when Tim smiled, he looked a little like Patrick Dempsey crossed with Guy Pierce. They drank red wine while she thought of movie stars and chocolate.

Later, the waiter interrupted the conversation as he placed the seafood platter that cost Christine more than a week's worth of groceries on the table. After she bit into the crab, she knew it was worth every penny. She felt alive with Tim and he put her at ease with his Harry Connick Jr. voice. "So tell me about you?" she asked.

"Now that's a complicated story and one that would take too long to tell over dinner."

"Come on. Give me something?"

"What do you want to know?"

"Do you have any brothers or sisters?"

"Nope. I was an only child."

"What about your parents? What are they like?"

"My father died in a car crash when I was five. My mother is a whole other story."

"I see that's a touchy subject. Another time."

"Well I know you're a detective, so we can skip that question. Tell me what you do to unwind?"

"Honestly Tim, other than the job I don't really do much. To be honest this is my first date this year."

"Oh, we'll have to change that now."

"You think so, huh?"

"So far I'm intrigued."

She bit into another piece of crab and her tongue was alive with the flavors of butter and garlic. Which she rinsed away with a swallow of wine.

"Where did you go to school?" she asked.

"Actually, after my Father died I spent most of my childhood at boarding schools and graduated from MIT."

"No way! So you're funny and smart."

The part that struck Christine the most was not that he graduated from MIT, but how his voice changed when he said he had spent his childhood in boarding schools. It sounded hollow. The cop in her told her to dig into it and ask more questions but if she wanted to see him again she thought she better not.

"Glad you think so. So you've been dateless in Manhattan for a year. What about before that? Anything long term?"

"Can't say I've had much luck there. Most men couldn't stomach the job. What about you?"

"I just haven't found the right one either. It seems women disappear after the first few dates."

"Well I guess the two of us are lucky that we found each other," she laughed.

Other diners ate and left but they stayed well past the main course. The Strip House had a way of making people lose track of time and money.

She felt his finger as it brushed her hand and rest on top of hers for the time it took to fill the glass. She wondered if they would kiss tonight. She wanted to. Christine was just about to say something when her Blackberry went off. She pulled it out of her purse and read the caller I.D.

"Sorry Tim, it's the office I have to take it."

"No problem."

"They what?" Christine said into the phone.

She listened intently. She could feel the heat rush to her face as the words hit home. Her stomach tightened. She looked over at Tim and he was staring back at it her with a more curious look then one of concern.

"Ok, I will be right there."

"Tim, I'm sorry, but I have to go."

"Really, what happened?" Tim asked.

"They found a body. An Agent that I work with. He's dead."

"Oh my God. Are you ok?"

"No, I have to go. Can you call me tomorrow?"

"Of course."

She got up from the table, turned around, and left.

***

The sidewalk was busy with bystanders. All whispering and pointing up at the flagpole draped in black plastic that shimmered from the floodlights, and crowded together as if they were attending the rights at a black mass. Desperate for a sacrifice. Desperate for the unveiling.

Tim stood against the cold grey building, blending in amongst the crowd.

He had followed Christine to the crime scene. The temptation tonight left him boiling and overflowing with urges. She had been different from the others. He couldn't place it. He was at odds with himself. The night built up a hunger that he couldn't forget and he needed her. He needed to take control of her. The power she held over him was sensational and awful at the same time. Her voice was strong and it conveyed authority. It was like the taste of bold coffee.

He watched as he stood in the back, behind the spectators and looked through the emergency vehicles on the street.

"Stay back, get back!" an officer said.

Officers pushed back the crowd and stretched yellow tape along the edge of the sidewalk. One of the officers pushed a woman hard enough to cause her to stumble.

"I said get back!"

Her eyes opened wide and her mouth gaped letting out a gasp. Tim avoided eye contact and instead found Christine standing beside another detective. His arm was wrapped around her. *Should be mine*, he thought. The two detectives stared up at the firefighter on the extension ladder. He was attempting to remove the body.

In the crowd a man screamed out, "Look there's an arm!" as he pointed toward the black plastic—*an arm indeed.* It hung down flapping against the ladder's metal frame. The firefighter heard the shouting and snuck the arm back underneath the plastic. The crowd roared.

The firefighter gripped the cutters and squeezed. The tip of the cutter bit hard into the chain that was looped over the flagpole.

Tim thought he heard a grunt from the firefighters' efforts but he couldn't be sure because of the noise coming from the crowd. The cutters bit through the first of the two chains holding up the body and banged against the flagpole. The firefighter attempted to regain his footing but it was too late; gravity took over, and he slipped back. He dropped the cutters and they fell against the steel ladder. His arm jutted out to grasp the railing and instead of steadying himself, he ripped the plastic off of the body. The roaring crowd went silent.

The body swung on the flagpole. The sight was eerie and the Tim could hear the scraping sound of the chain against the pole. The victim's hair hanging toward the sidewalk below. It was wet from blood and reflecting crimson. Streaks of red covered the body and the victim's eyes were wide open. Christine's scream carried over the silent crowd.

"Cover him up, God damn it!" she said.

The firefighter regained his footing and covered the body and the crowd quieted again. Christine's arm was flailing up in the direction of the firefighter.

She looked back at the crowd. Her eyes were full of rage. Tim watched on. The firefighter climbed down the ladder with the wrapped body slung over his shoulder.

The red steel gurney held the weight of the body as he placed it down.

Three NYC Medical Examiner staff ushered the body into the back of a white van. Their black jumpsuits looked faded in the bright lights. The door opened and inside two levels divided the light-blue interior. The MEs wheeled the gurney back and slammed into the back of the vehicle. The legs collapsed, the gurney slid in and the MEs slammed the doors shut.

Tim turned away from the commotion and drifted up the sidewalk and away from Christine.

On the corner, two blocks down Seventy-Second, Tim approached a black SUV. Whoever was in there would have a clear view of the action. As he got closer, a head appeared in the dark interior and filled out the top half of the windshield. White-eyes peered back through the glass. Not at Tim, but at the scene. Not once did the pair of eyes turn in his direction.

As he passed the passenger-side-window, the full size of the man came into view. His chest stuck out like the grill of a truck. His powerful looking hands gripped the steering wheel and Tim could hear classical music seeping from the trucks interior. He understood the look and he knew it well: the hunger and admiration. A job well done. Tim was thinking he could possibly be looking at The Picasso Killer.

He waited until he was well past the vehicle's line of sight and punched the plate-number into his Blackberry.

***

Lawson looked on from a safe distance and in the comfort of his SUV. The scene was alive with wondrous commotion. His most recent display of "Michael" earned him his own respect. Saint Seans, "Dense Macabre" played through the speakers and filled the interior with an eerie sound setting the mood as Lawson's play enfolded three blocks down the street. It was difficult to make out Christine and Jeffries but they were there.

He felt nothing in the way of emotions for either of the detectives. Michael would never have been part of his selection pool but the agent presented himself in such a manner that Lawson could not ignore the calling.

Michael was his fourth presentation and it would be his last until Lawson was cleared from the investigation.

The usage of the Egyptian rope was risky. He knew that. Still, it felt like just the right addition to his masterpiece for the St. Patrick's addition. How quickly they tied it back to him was unnerving. Markus Heilbronner the victim deserved something original. Special. He was a man that Lawson met on a hunting trip. A brief encounter that would later cost him his life. Mark, that night, drank to the point where common sense eluded him. It was a passing of sorts but one Lawson would remember. Mark finished his last drink of the night. The bar at the hunting lodge was closing for the evening and as he wobbled through the maze of sofas, he slipped and fell toward Lawson. He reacted swiftly and stopped Mark before he landed on top of him. What angered Lawson was not the sour breath coming from the man's open mouth, it was the slight brushing of the front of their bodies, and he felt the man's penis rub against his own. The thought irked him and he wanted to kill Mark at that moment, instead, he planned something very special indeed. After learning about his messy divorce with a beautiful Egyptian woman, Lawson could not pass up the irony of using the ropes.

As Lawson watched the MEs drive off with Michaels corpse he thought about the display, which Lawson named "Half of a Man" was inspired by the victims own glass is half-empty attitude.

Lawson noticed the man coming toward the SUV. He looked briefly at the pedestrian and moved his attention back to the players in costume.

TWENTY-ONE

"Damn it, Jeffries this hits too close to home." Christine said.

"I know what you mean. It's crazy. Look; I jazzed the guy but I didn't hate him."

"I need a minute. Tell the captain I'll be right back"

She moved along the row of desks to the hallway and into the women's washroom. The concrete walls were painted a light shade of beige. Six stalls the color of eggshell lined the wall closest to her. She opened the last stall, pulled up her dress, pulled down her pantyhose, and sat on the toilet. She cried as she peed.

She flushed the toilet and re-adjusted herself.

At the sink, she ran the hot water from the tap and splashed the water on her face. She looked into the mirror. Tiny rivers streamed down her face and her eyes looked like a raccoon's eyes. The night that started off so well and had ended so horrifically. She liked being a cop but hated the bodies. She could never get over the bodies; and the image of Michael's torso hanging from the flagpole was seared permanently in her mind. She filled her palm with soap and scrubbed what was left of her make-up from her face. She hated wearing make-up.

Christine entered the captain's office and Jeffries was already seated in the far chair.

"Christine, we have to talk."

She met his eyes and she felt exhausted.

"Are you ok?" The captain asked, as Christine sat down.

"No."

She hadn't respected Michael but his murder left her feeling a deep loss. She knew in her gut that Lawson was good for it. This was a hard blow and her heart sunk to the pit of her stomach. She felt vomit at the back of her throat and gulped it back down. She rubbed her face and her fingers flowed through her raven hair. She threw her head back and collapsed into the chair. The captain pulled a bottle of rye out of his drawer, poured three glasses, slid one to Jeffries, and handed one to Christine, which she accepted.

She stared at the captain as he swallowed the brown fire. The glass clinked on the bottom row of his teeth. She followed the motion and downed the two-fingered serving.

"Christine, I received a call from the mayor's office ten minutes ago. You're not going to like this, but you need to know this is out of my hands."

"I'm not going to like what?"

"I tried to back you on this one but with Michael...well, let's just say that there is one pissed off Director at the FBI."

"What's out of your hands?"

"The case, Christine... we've lost the case."

"No way Captain! We're closing in on Lawson. We're close."

"The Bureau's bringing in the big guns—we're done."

"This is my case and this isn't their jurisdiction. It's bad enough that Michael was included. We had it under control and he just wanted his name added to the credits. Now they want to take over the damn thing. They have no right!"

"This is coming down from the top; it's out of my hands. They will be here first thing in the morning. I need you and Jeffries to stay and organize the case files. Use Crystal...whatever you need. Just make sure it's clean."

"I don't need help. The files are spotless."

"Detective, I mean it. No holes. You will need to be here first thing for a briefing. After that, you'll be reassigned to another case."

"What case?"

"We found a body last week. Looks like a rape gone bad. The victim was a young female. Her parents found her in her apartment. Seems she hadn't showed up to work for three days. The dad was worried and came down. That's when he found her. She was naked on her bed and stabbed twelve times. The visual messed him up. We need a win on this one, Christine. Talk to Crystal and she'll update you on the rest of the details. Jeffries, you good with this?"

"Ok Captain, but this sucks," Jeffries said

Christine said nothing. Instead, she gripped the wooden arms of the chair and pushed up. She wrenched the handle, opened the door, and walked out.

TWENTY-TWO

Two years on the case and now, it was ripped out from underneath her. It wasn't right. The FBI didn't care about the hours she had invested. The all nighters—the emotional investment. *This was bullshit.* She scanned her living room and it was a mess. With the case, and the date with Tim, she had no time to do her weekly ritual. The sun was shining through her window and the yellow-rays highlighted dust bunnies under the sofa. More dust along the end tables. She walked into her bedroom. Her housecoat was still on top of her bed where she left it, the day before.

Her second wind kicked in and she cleaned. She cleaned.

Cleaned.

Two hours passed, and sweat soaked her forehead. All she could smell was pine. The kitchen sparkled. She even cleaned the crumbs from the bottom of the toaster. She felt refreshed and renewed and all she needed now was a hot shower.

The phone rang. It was Tim and she was happy to hear his voice.

"Hey, is everything ok?" Tim asked.

"No, actually, but I don't want to unload on you. So thanks for asking. Sorry about cutting our date short."

"I'm worried about you."

"I'll be alright. It's part of the job. Just hits harder when it's another cop."

"I see."

"Thanks again for understanding. I did have a really good time on our date and I hope I haven't scared you off."

"Me too. And no, I'm not scared yet. Should we try again?"

"Definitely. What are you doing next weekend?"

"Well...It's probably way too soon but how would you feel about coming up to my cottage in the Catskills?" he asked.

"Umm..."

Any other time she would laugh at the request. She would have said *Are you crazy, we just met.* She would have explained that they didn't know each other yet. She would have turned him down flat. Not today. Today the offer sounded great. Just what she needed. He had a way of explaining things that made her feel completely at ease.

"So you'll come?"

She hesitated for just another second.

"Sure, I haven't been to the Catskills since I was kid."

"Great! I'll pick you up Friday night. We'll drive up after rush hour."

"Ok, thanks Tim. See you then."

The phone call ended and blood flowed, her heart filled and released. She felt the beat in her chest. Her head was a little swimmy and she felt a little lighter than before the call.

She entered the bathroom and it reminded her of a Russian bathhouse. Steam filled every corner of the room... She forgot she was running the shower.

TWENTY-THREE

The Audi hummed along as Christine sat in the passenger seat. The coffee cup was still warm in her hand even though they had been driving just over an hour. The traffic had put up a fight getting out of Manhattan, but now that they were out on Hwy 87, the roads were less congested.

"So, how do you feel?" he said.

"Better. It's like déjà vu. The drive I mean."

"Yeah, I get that. I feel it every time I make the turn on to 87. Something in my mind switches and I swear I can almost smell the pine needles."

"You really love it up there, huh?"

"Wait till you see the place. If there ever was a heaven that's what it would look like."

"Well heaven described by my father looks like pearly gates sitting on top of white fluffy clouds. Does it look anything like that?" Christine joked.

"Ever been to Kaaterskill Falls?" he asked.

"You know, I think so; but it's been so long I can't remember."

"Oh, you would remember. We'll go there tomorrow, you will love it!"

She met his eyes and they were soft. The look had her feeling light again. The whole idea of getting out of the city and away for a few days was exciting. She was happy she made the decision to go. His description of the cottage was so detailed; she could still picture it in her mind. He told her it was as if someone lifted a home from Malibu Beach and slammed into the side of the mountain.

Dark wood panels lined the outer walls: slits in the wall of wood formed six windows—two in the front, two in the back, and one on each of the sides. The balcony on the far corner had a stairway that led up to the rooftop patio. From the roof, you had a three-hundred-and-sixty-degree view of the mountain and the reservoir below. She couldn't wait.

"Hey, I have to go pee. Can you pull over soon?"

"Sure. There's a restaurant coming up that serves an All-Day-Breakfast. We can stop there. You hungry?"

"I could eat something."

"Cool. Then greasy spoon it is."

He smiled at her and the dimples on his cheeks matched the one in the bottom of his chin. She admired the rough look of his skin and she returned a smile as he took the next exit.

The entrance to the restaurant was to the right of the exit and only two other cars were parked in the lot. A white Chevy Cavalier with rust crusted around the wheel wells and a pickup truck with a missing tailgate. The worn bed liner held a red toolbox that was snug against a piece of two-by-four that ran the width of the bed.

She opened the car door and rushed out. The stones crunched under her feet as she scurried to the door of the restaurant. The bell attached to the door rang as she pushed it open. The waitress behind the bar shot Christine a warm smile.

"Bathroom?"

"To the left Darlin."

The bathroom, thank God, was empty.

As she re-entered the dining area of the restaurant, she noticed Tim sitting in a booth in the back corner. She walked toward the booth minus the large latte and felt lighter.

"Thank you." She said to the waitress as she passed.

"No problem Darlin. When you gotta go, God couldn't stop ya. Bless the Lord." The waitress made the sign of the cross.

The old counter top was lined with chrome napkin containers. Christine felt nostalgic and thought the only thing missing was a jukebox. She slid into the booth across from Tim. Steam rose from the two coffee cups in front of her.

"Feel better?"

She smiled back at him and blood rushed to her cheeks. She took a sip of the coffee. It was bitter and black.

"Much better now thanks."

'Rumble' sung by Link Wray played from the small radio that sat on top of the glass case filled with an assortment of pies.

Tim handed her a menu.

"I know what I want. You want to have a look. The eggs are a little greasy but they taste good."

"Yeah. You've had them before I take it."

"Been here a few times on the way to the cottage. It's usually quiet—and you have to love Elma."

"She's always working?"

"Yep, owns the place. Nearly forty years."

"Hmm," Christine looked over the menu and deciding what she would have was easy: not much to choose from.

Elma arrived at the table and pulled a note pad from the pocket of her stained apron.

"So what'll it be, folks."

"I'll have the fruit bowl and some brown toast please."

Tim ordered eggs with sides of brown toast and bacon.

"...and to drink?"

Christine ordered grapefruit juice and Tim ordered the same. He looked at her, his right eyebrow raised slightly.

"No eggs?"

"Not for me. I don't think my stomach could take the grease."

The waitress shot her a stern look.

"Who said my eggs were greasy?" She looked down at Tim and gave him a slap on the shoulder. "Bugger."

Later, when they drove past the reservoir, she did think she was in heaven. The lake was serene. It reflected back a cataract of white clouds mixed in a blue sky. The steep incline of the mountain gave her the feeling of falling. Then the roar of the Audi's engine filled her ears and they climbed the escarpment.

Tim had been accurate in his description of the cottage. It was a modern building amongst a majestic mountain range.

"Tim it's beautiful."

"I know what you mean...beats the metal and concrete huh?"

"It sure does. Thank you again for the invite."

Inside the cottage, oak cabinets framed the stainless steel appliances to the right in the open kitchen.

"Oh my god! The place is amazing. The kitchen is bigger than my apartment."

He turned toward her and took the bag from her hand.

"Hey follow me. I'll show you your room."

They walked through the open room to a spiral staircase in the back corner. *My own room hmmm. Not bad. Not bad at all.* She would have easily slept in the same bed with him, but this was a little different—respectful.

She climbed the iron stairs to the second level.

A short hallway held two doors; one, she assumed, was the master bedroom because the other one he opened.

He placed her bag on a bed that was high enough that she hoped she didn't roll off it in her sleep.

"This is your room. There's a bathroom with a shower. No bath sorry." He pointed to the door off to the right. "There's a closet in there. You'll find an extra blanket on the top shelf, but I doubt you'll be cold. It gets really hot up here when the fireplace is on."

"Tim, it's wonderful."

"I'm going to put my stuff away. I'll be up the hall when you're done in here."

"Ok, thanks."

She unpacked her bag and laid everything out on the bed. She took her toiletries out, walked into the bathroom. The shower stall looked new. She placed her toothbrush in the ceramic cup on the sink.

The dresser on the far side of the room held six drawers. She placed her clothes on top of the dresser.

Out in the hallway, she could hear him in the next room. She walked through the large doorframe and into the open room. She remembered seeing a balcony coming into the cottage. The railing ran the length of the room and from the floor to the top rail round posts jutted up like wooden teeth.

He was pulling a sweater over his bare chest, and she caught a glimpse of his flat stomach. She turned her head and focused her attention on a large wooden desk at the far end. She could see the apple emblem on the cover of the laptop that sat alone on top of desk.

"Hey, what do you think?"

"Tim, this place must have cost you a mint."

"I wasn't too concerned with cash. I wanted something that I could live in. A little get-away, if you know what I mean."

"Tim, this is more than a 'little get-away'."

"Care for a drink?"

"Sure!"

Downstairs, they talked as the bottle of wine emptied. The fire crackled and the heat felt nice on her skin.

"So I lost the Picasso Case." After the words left her mouth, she wished she could have caught them in mid-flight and thrown them in the fire.

"No way. What happened?"

"It's a long story."

"We have lots of time."

"The FBI is taking over the case."

"Why would they do that?"

"Michael Roberts was an FBI agent. He was the guy that was murdered and if they lose one of their own well..."

"You're kidding?"

"I wish I wasn't. When I first found out that he was assisting us on the case, I was pissed. We didn't want the FBI's help. The case was coming along fine."

"So, why was he there?"

"It seems, from what I could gather that he was looking to add his name to the credits when we nailed Picasso."

"It's disgusting how the media names the killers and exploits the victims to increase their ratings."

"Yeah no kidding. In fact, that's why he was there. The case was so well publicized that if his name was linked to the capture, more than likely he would've received a promotion."

"Sounds like it was all political."

"Yep. Now I'm on a new case"

"Really, what's that about?"

"Listen, I shouldn't be telling you any of this,"

"If you don't want to, don't worry about it. Although now you've got me interested," he said.

"It's a murder case. The girl was raped."

"Shit, what happened?"

"The father found her. He was devastated. Anyway I don't have too much to go on right now I just got the case."

She looked at him and he seemed to be lost in thought. He must have noticed her staring because he smiled.

"Christ! Sorry, but that's awful," he said.

"Let's change the subject."

He poured the rest of the wine into her glass. He left her on the sofa and walked into the kitchen. She could see him pull a foil package out of the freezer and place it the oven.

He returned carrying another bottle of red wine. He filled his glass and sat down beside her on the sofa.

"Let's toast to us."

His eyes met hers and they slanted ever so slightly. She peered in deeper and tried to pull something out, but all she could see was his warm blue-grey eyes staring back. She slid her hand behind his neck and kissed him. It was their first kiss. It was nice to feel his soft lips.

"What was that for?" he asked.

"You looked like you needed that."

They finished the dinner that consisted of lasagna that was delicious but was too filling and a garden salad mixed with fresh vegetables. She noticed him looking at his watch and she held her breath. She felt like the night was ending and she didn't want it to. She looked at her own watch and it was only 9:30.

"I want to show you something. Come on."

He grabbed both their glasses and gave her arm a soft tug. She moved with him through the room, up the staircase, down the hall, and out the patio door.

Outside, the cool mountain air brought goose bumps to the back of her arms. He led her up one more flight of stairs to the rooftop. He walked her past the hot tub and over to the loungers. Tim flipped the switch on the outdoor heater. With a poof, the screen turned from silver to red. She could feel the heat instantly wash over her.

"Sit down" he said.

She did. The cold plastic cover stole the heat from her ass and she arched her back in response. He laid down beside her and checked his watch again.

"What is it? Why do you keep checking your watch?" she asked.

"Just look up. Any second now."

The sky was the darkest of black and littered with flashing white specs. The only clouds she could see were far off in the distant mountains. Then it was there. Like magic. Like a sleight of hand trick. A long trail of light the size of a ruler floated across the night sky. The front ball screamed white and mixtures of blues and purples writhed within the tail creating a small streak in the night sky.

"It's a meteor shower," he said.

"It's amazing! I've never seen one before." And as quickly as the words left her mouth it was gone. It seemed to have reflected off the earth's atmosphere and set off in a different direction.

"That was truly incredible. How did you know?"

"I read about it online. Cool, huh?" he said.

The night ended with Tim tucking her in and kissing her softly. She would have slept with him but she was glad he was taking his time. She was starting to fall for him. He closed the door and the light slipped from the room as if sucked by a vacuum. She shut her eyes and sleep found her.

TWENTY-FOUR

The events the previous night played out according to Tim's plan. She was moving slower than most women would under those circumstances but the kiss was a good start. He recognized the indicators, the small things most men don't pay attention to; like how many times she touched her hair or like the way her knees pointed toward him as she spoke.

Christine was the only one that he has ever taken to the cottage. He liked that she was here—in his domain.

He heard her walking about upstairs as the echoed footsteps came from the floorboards above. The hot grease popped from the pan and burned his wrist. He moved his attention back to the bacon and flipped the strips one by one. He cooked each strip evenly to be the perfect color and texture. He heard her voice call out. Turning his head, he saw her beautiful wide smile spread across her face and reveal her straight white teeth. She was definitely a morning person. He loved that she could go without make-up. She was naturally beautiful. She leaned over the railing and her white tank top floated over the banister. Her toned arms on the rail and he liked how sculpted they looked.

"Hey."

"Morning sleepy-head—hungry?" he asked.

"Famished. It smells great. Whatcha cookin?"

"Bacon."

Her smile was infectious and he smiled back up at her. Her black hair hung to the right side of her face. It was a shame that all this beauty will go to waste.

"I'm gonna take a shower."

"Ok, take your time. Hey."

Her head turned back around and their eyes met.

"You're definitely a morning person. You look great." He said.

"Why thank you. You look good yourself."

He watched her turn with a flick of her hair and she moved out of view.

The breakfast was done and so was the coffee. He filled two thermoses and handed one to Christine.

"You're gonna need it."

They headed out to the car. The air was crisp and a white blanket covered the mountain slope. Christine held him by the waist and kissed the back of his neck. He was really going to enjoy this. Fire raced through his veins and at the same time, something itched inside him.

The drive for the most part was quiet. She seemed to be lost in thought or in the mountain scenery. Whatever it was, he welcomed the silence. A small triangle moved up as the GPS reset as they drove through the town of Palenville. His current location glowed white. A town so small that with a blink and breath you would pass through it.

It took forty minutes to drive to the Kaaterskill parking area off Route 23. He parked in a small section of road that was not an official parking lot. It was more like a worn patch on the ground made from hiking enthusiasts. On a Sunday morning and in the off-season the place would be deserted. Snow floated down and as he turned off the ignition, the first few flakes that landed on the hood melted away.

Outside, he handed her a walking stick from the trunk and swung a backpack over his shoulder. They were both wearing layered clothing as he had suggested. Tim wore an expensive pair of hiking boots and she was wearing a pair of running shoes. Tim had checked the treads and he told Christine they would be fine but to be careful.

He closed the trunk and it clicked in place. With a press of the remote, the car locked.

The trail started to the right of Bastion Falls and as they passed the falls, he studied her. She stopped and stared up at the cold blue water splashing white off the rocks.

"Is this it?" she said.

He laughed and gave her a pat on the ass.

"Keep moving. It's another hour or so down the trail. That's just a baby compared to Kaaterskill." He motioned in the direction of the path entrance.

Three hundred yards in, the maintained path started to thin out and the trek became more laborious. Rocks, tree stumps, and scattered branches led the way into the rocky trail. He could feel his breathing quicken.

"How you doin back there?"

"I love it."

Her response came back unlabored; her voice was clear.

"Watch your step. The trunks can be a little slippery."

Clumps of snow weighed down the branches above and white shapes from his distance looked like small white owls waiting to swoop down. He moved along, his legs worked hard and he could feel the muscles warming in his quads.

The view ahead gave way to a long strip of forest with hibernating trees. The snow-covered ground crunched under his feet. He stopped and Christine almost ran him over. Her arms draped around his middle and she squeezed.

"Thank you for bringing me here. It's exhilarating."

As he turned toward her, their eyes met for a moment in the cold forest and he kissed her. She responded, pulling on his bottom lip. Her upper lip was wet with sweat and he could taste the salty delicious liquid.

"Thirsty?" he asked.

"Yes."

He pulled two bottles of water out the backpack and handed one to her. They both took long swallows.

"How much farther?" she asked.

"It's just up over that hill—another five minutes." He pointed to the incline ahead of them.

Tim was ahead of her by only a yard or so, leading her down a deep incline along the escarpment. He knew the path well and he was taking them in the right direction. His heartbeat was rhythmic and his blood rushed through his veins feeding nutrients to his hot muscles. She followed behind driving like a locomotive and he liked her attitude; that she was in great shape.

He inhaled the cold air into his lungs.

"Ok it's not far now, just over the ridge," he said.

"I think I can hear it!" she said.

"It will leave you breathless, trust me."

She followed him up the ridge and he heard it. It was almost deafening. It was as if static noise from a thousand televisions roared back. The angry water filled his ears with its drumming sound as it crashed into the rocks below.

Trees ran along both sides of the stream. The expelled water from the falls raced down the mountain eroding the stones in its path. The green leaves were long gone and empty branches reaching toward the sky shone from the frozen mist that covered them. The air became dense and he felt the wetness wash over him like a thousand bee stings. He closed his eyes and let it sooth him. He hungered for the pain.

He turned and smiled as she walked into the opening, Christine looked so beautiful. She seemed at peace from the surroundings. The wetness covered her jacket and her hair. Her hair was the color of a raven; mist froze to the black strands like the branches of the trees. She looked angelic.

He wanted to have her now. He wanted to hold her down and touch her. He wanted her to fight back hard and resist. There wouldn't be a single person around to hear her scream. All of his nerves fired at a once and he felt as though he were burning. He thought he must have been glowing. She rushed him fast and he stumbled back and almost lost his footing. They both would have ended up soaked from the chilled water behind them. His hiking boot gripped wet stones, its rubber teeth clamped hard and he stabilized.

She held him tight and kissed him. Her eyes closed and her lashes felt wet.

"This is Kaaterskill falls huh? WOW! Oh my God it's fantastic," she said.

He regained his composure.

"You almost killed us." He pointed to the rushing current behind him. She laughed and her hand rushed to her mouth. Her eyes flickered.

"Oh shit. Sorry," she shrugged her shoulders.

"Let's go! Wait until you see the view from the foot of the falls."

She walked beside him as they made the hike down the path. He had to help her a few times to make it over the slippery rocks. The two-tiered falls carved its way down about a redwood tree's distance from the top. At the mouth, a beard of cold blue ice formed and jagged stalactites hung from the bottom of the frozen rock on the cliff. The rushing water boomed and he watched as gravity pulled at the water creating formations in the ice. The frozen mass created a cave formation at the back of the falls. *Perfect.* They were alone.

"Come over here, I want to show you something," he said.

She arrived at his side and he pointed to the cave behind the falls. His voice was a mere whisper over the roar of crashing water.

"Let's check it out."

He navigated his way around a large boulder and he was moving close to the edge. Her hand slipped off his waist. *Close now. Almost there.*

It happened fast. He felt the world turn on its axis and he was sliding.

Whoa. Whoa, Shit. He was falling fast down the side of the bank. The side of his wrist slammed hard into a rock and the pain was instant.

"Tim," she screamed.

He hit the bottom of the ice and his ankle rolled over. Then the pop. He felt the pulsing sensation flood to his ankle. It throbbed.

"Tim, oh my God. Are you ok?"

She stood above him on the white ice. *How could he have been so stupid? So clumsy—fuck!* He tried to rotate his foot. It was painful, but he could move it. He felt his ankle with his hands and it was swelling. Soon it would be the size of a softball. Shit. Shit. Shit. He felt the back of his head and there was warm sticky fluid. He pressed hard and there didn't seem to be any flow. He must have cut his head during the fall.

"Tim, are you ok?"

"Yeah, I think so. My ankle feels like it's sprained. I can move it so nothing is broken. I think."

"Can you make it up?"

He looked to his left; the water's edge was a few feet in front of him. To the right was a solid wall of ice. To his left, the bank veered down. There was a rock outcropping, and Christine was scaling the rocks. The pain in his head flooded as if the falls were expelling pots and pans instead of water. He winced.

She was at his side within seconds and was helping him to his feet. He slipped again and put pressure on his ankle. He grunted and placed his arm around her for support.

She guided him up the icy path and she followed behind as he pulled himself up the rocks. She trailed with her hand firm on his lower back for support. They both made the climb without any other slips or falls. She sat beside him on a large boulder.

"You really gave me a scare back there. Are you ok?"

"Yeah, it took me for a little spin. Hey, thanks for your help."

She wrapped her arm around his shoulder and gave him a squeeze. "Anytime" she said.

They both laughed.

"Are you going to be able to make it out?"

He could tell she was serious about the question.

"I should be ok. I need to put some ice on it to bring down the swelling. Then, with you to lean on, I should be good."

Below him, she was gathering snow in her hand. The cold hit fast and bit at his skin as she placed it on his ankle.

"This ok?" she said.

"Hey, you don't have to do that."

"It's ok really, it's no problem."

She held it there on his ankle and her other hand reached underneath his pant leg, massaging the back of his calf. He was fighting with himself to control his urges. Ten minutes ago, he was going to rape and kill this woman and now she was taking care of *him*. It was all too strange. *Stretch it out. Another Time.*

They sat long enough that he couldn't feel his butt beneath him, and then he grabbed her hand.

"We came all this way, I think we should at least take a look," he said.

"You sure?"

"I'll lean on you and use the walking stick. It'll be ok, I promise. Let's go."

They both walked in stride toward the entrance to the cave. He used the stick to support his right foot. The walls of the cave were porcelain white and gleamed with hints of blue. The water rushed over the lip of the cave as they moved along the back wall. The sound crashed around him and it was deafening. She pulled him into her. Behind the ice, he kissed her. First, soft sucking on her bottom lip and nibbling. Then harder. Their mouths opened and the heat from her warmed his cheek. He was hot, his urgency soaked him, and it was written on her face as well. Her hands were exploring and pulling on him. Reaching under his jacket. Under his sweater. On his skin. They were cold, then not. Her nails dug into him and she kissed him. Her hands reappeared from underneath his clothes.

She stopped.

She grasped his arms by the biceps and pushed a few inches away from him.

"Wow! That was...wow."

He stood there staring down at her, both their chests heaving.

"We should get going," she said.

With that, she guided him out of the cave. He was swimming in emotion and his head was spinning. *What had just happened?*

The hike back was hell and took a lot longer than the trip up to the falls. They had to stop every ten minutes so they could both rest. She was incredible and resilient, like a workhorse.

***

On the patio, he switched on the heat lamps and took the cover off the hot tub. He dropped his housecoat and slid into the soothing hot water. It was a perfect 102 degrees. His muscles reacted within seconds, a few quick spasms, and then the release. All the tension melted away like snow that landed on a heat lamp.

She approached the tub wearing one of his bathrobes. It hung from her shoulder and looked too big for her. She was holding a tray in her left hand and two glasses and an opened bottle of Mondovi in the other. He knew which bottle. It was from the reserve stock. "Hey, looks like you brought us some treats," he said.

"We deserve it."

She placed the items on the side of the hot tub and handed him the bottle. The robe dropped off her shoulders. Her round white breasts glowed in the moonlight. Her small nipples fired out from the cold. The moment was serene. Then the robe was on the railing and she slid into the tub with the suit she was born in.

He poured the wine, handed her a glass and they soaked in the tub. They finished the tray, which consisted of Caciocavallo cheese, slices of honey ham, and thin crackers. They picked at the tray while exchanging hungered glances. The second glass had his head floating. The alcohol thinned his blood and combined with the heat from the hot tub he was dizzy.

"I had an amazing time today. Well, except for your fall, that is."

"Me too, except for the fall."

They both laughed.

Her eyes changed to a more serious expression and she placed her glass on the wood stairs. She floated toward him. Her hair was wet and steam rose from the top of her head. Her skin shone and she floated up onto his lap. Her breasts pressed up against his chest as she pulled herself against him. She kissed his mouth; with the pressure still lingering she slid around to his neck and bit down on it. He could feel her shaking against him. She moved in a fluid motion as her hands rubbed his back and shoulders. His cock responded from all the attention and he could feel it pressing against her stomach. *Fuck, she moved fast.* Her hand was around it and stroking it. Her mouth was on his again. She was anxious and hungry; he could feel it in her kisses and her hand that pulled on his cock. She rose up and the hot water dripped from her breasts. He reached up and squeezed them. His mouth shot to the right breast and he sucked hard. He tongued the bottom of her breast, licked up to her nipple, and bit down. She arched her back and with her hand still on his cock rubbed it back and forth on her pussy. After the fourth swipe, she sat down on it and it felt tight. She let out a soft groan.

"Hmmmm. Fuck," she said.

She rocked back on him and he pushed up into her. Her thighs rose and fell in rhythm and the movement was hurried. He felt like he had the urge to rush. Her breasts slapped on to his chest. He tangled his hand into the back of her hair and pushed harder into her. Her groaning was getting louder. She shifted and he felt the tip of his cock rub up against something deep inside her. Every time he pushed up and she sat down, she let out a sigh. Her hand pulled against his neck and he could feel the strain of the muscle.

"Ahhh... Fuck," she moaned.

She dropped on him and her hot body slipped against his. Water sprayed up and splashed both their faces.

He pushed her off and to the side pulling her over to the stairs. Steam floated up in a thin fog as the water soaked the cold wood, which created a film of slick sheen that reflected back the moon's image. It was cold and she was half way out of the tub. Her breasts squished against the wet wood as she pulled the robe toward her. He slid into her from behind. She was warm inside as he moved in and out of her. The robe under her head muffled her groans. The steam rose from his chest, he rocked back and forth first slow then faster. He felt the urge to rush again and he pushed into her one last time.

He pulled back and she turned around to face him and kissed him. Her arms draped over his shoulders.

His ankle throbbed.

TWENTY-FIVE

Jeffries hesitated as he reached for the door to his apartment. Dread washed over and stuck to him. It felt tacky. The fighting, lately, wore on him. He placed his hand on the door knob and the cold metal cooled his palm. He rested his other hand on the door frame, slouched over, and exhaled giving in to defeat.

He opened the door and closed it behind him. As he entered the hallway he noticed that the faded white paint on the wall needed a fresh coat. That was another fight on a different day. Last year Teresa had asked him to paint the apartment and now the wall was just another reminder of the broken promises he made. He placed his coat on the empty wooden peg that hung on the wall. The hooks where Teresa's and Sarah's coats should have been were empty.

Slamming sounds coming from the bedroom, bounced off the walls, and into his ears. The feeling of the inevitable confrontation cooked inside him. A bottle of Jim Beam called to him from the kitchen. He answered.

In the kitchen, he grabbed a glass from the cupboard and emptied the last of the brown gold liquid into it. A stinging sensation tickled the back of his throat as he drank the alcohol down.

The closet door in the bedroom squeaked open and the scraping sound of hangers biting into the metal drove spikes in the back of his head. Fuck.

As he passed the bathroom, he could see that only his toothbrush was in the cup. Teresa rushed out of the bedroom and he froze. His back stiffened and he held his breath. He tried to speak but all that came out was "uggg." She stopped and stared up at him. He could smell the sweat. It was strong. Her pink cotton shirt was drenched underneath her breasts.

The silence between them unnerved him. She looked ambitious. Her eyes told him all he needed to know. They were cold. He wanted to say something. Instead, he shuffled his feet on the carpet. The track marks left from the vacuum were still imbedded and he passed his foot over top erasing the marks in the carpet.

"I've had it," Teresa said.

"Had it with what?"

She shook her head and moved away. Her shoulders slouched as she turned and walked past him. He followed her into the living room. He could see lights glowing from the building across the street through their living room window. The white drapes looked clean. The house always looked clean.

"Come on. Let's just sit down and talk about it."

"Oh, now you want to talk."

Jeffries threw his hands up into the air and turned his back on his wife.

"What the fuck is wrong with you! Why are you always doing this?" he said.

"Look, I don't want to fight with you anymore. I just can't take it. It's like living with a dead person. You come home at all hours of the night. You don't tell me anything. You just plop yourself in front of the TV and zone out."

"You know what I do and where I am. What are you talking about?"

"That's just it. I don't know. You don't tell me anything. You never did. So no, I don't know."

Jeffries walked into the kitchen, opened up the refrigerator, and took out a beer. Her footsteps echoed his and as he turned, she was just inches away.

"Great! Now you're going to drink. Perfect."

"What is your problem?"

"What's my problem? You're my problem! This marriage is my fucking problem!"

The frustration consumed him. He didn't know what to say to calm her down. She was losing it.

"What are you saying?" he said.

"I don't know what I'm saying. All I know is that I need to get away from here. I'm going to my sisters and I'm taking Sarah with me."

The words struck home, stopped him from pacing across the carpet.

"What are you talking about?"

"I've already called my sister. She's expecting us."

"So that's it?"

"Yep."

"Fine, fuck it. Go then."

As Teresa turned, the strained look on her face faded and disappointment reflected back at him. He followed her through the cramped hallway and into the bedroom. Two suitcases weighed down the bed.

The words that he needed were as usual locked away. Instead, he twisted the cap off the beer and swallowed half the bottle in one gulp.

"Teresa. Stop. Just stop for a second."

She moved the one suitcase off the bed. The brown leather handle looked big in her small hand and she struggled to place the suitcase on to the floor. The case bulged in the center and looked pregnant.

"Forget it," she said.

Outside in the hallway, he watched as Sarah opened her door. Tears ran down her face. It killed him. He bent down to meet her at her level and he hugged her. Her tiny arms wrapped around his neck. Her hair smelled like grape and watermelon.

"I'm sorry, Muffin."

"Daddy, why are you and Mommy fighting?"

"It's something adults do. Please don't cry."

It broke him, and it was hard to swallow. His heart hurt, which turned his sadness to hate and he redirected that emotion back toward Teresa.

The suitcase slammed into his hip as his wife pushed by.

"Come on, Sarah. We've talked about this. We're going to see Aunty Mary," she said.

"Is Daddy coming?"

"No. We talked about this. Now come on."

Jeffries removed his daughter's arms from around his neck and she stood there in the hallway looking up at him.

"Sarah, come on now," Teresa said.

Sarah shuffled out of the hallway and stopped one last time to look back at him. She looked confused and sad.

The next vision he saw was the door closing behind them. No sounds filled the apartment. Just silence.

TWENTY-SIX

The next morning Tim sat on the sofa while he arranged the two bowls of water on the floor: one warm and one cold.

"So this works, huh? Don't you think I should wrap it?"

"No. No. Just do as I said. Put your foot in the warm water first, then when you pull it out to put it in the cold, try to spell the alphabet with your toes. Trust me; you'll be walking in no time."

The warm water felt good on his skin. He rolled his foot around and it was still stiff.

After two minutes, he pulled it out of the water, pointed his leg out straight, and started with the letter *A, then B, then C...* "Hey this feels pretty good. Hurts a little, but I can feel it loosening up."

"Just keep doing it. It doesn't work right away, Silly." She laughed at him from the kitchen.

He could hear the sizzling eggs and the popping of bacon grease. The aroma of brewed coffee widened his nostrils. He placed his foot into the cold water and it felt as if he had stuck his bare foot into snow. It reminded him of the feeling he got when he struck his funny bone. His foot was tickling all over, which made him hit the side of the bowl with it and water spilled all over the hardwood. *Shit.*

"Hey, Christine. Can you pass me a towel."

She was already in mid-stride as he looked back up. She handed him the grey dishtowel. He placed it on the floor and the towel soaked up the water. As he scrubbed up the tiny pools of water, the cleaning sensation ignited a memory. The more he wiped, the more vivid the images appeared out of the darkness of his mind.

***

He was back in boarding school, two days after he lost his virginity. He felt safe in his dorm room. The cramped space soothed him and was familiar.

He stood next to his bed and pulled the poster of the racecar from the wall, crumpled it, and tossed it into the wastebasket. He replaced it with a poster of "The Shining" and held it in place by pushing tacks into the wall. He unrolled another poster "The Serpent and The Rainbow" and tacked it to the far wall.

He had made friends with the pimple-faced teenager at the local video store. Although Tim had six years to wait until his eighteenth birthday, the clerk looked past that fact and let him rent restricted movies. He liked the sex scenes in the "The Serpent and The Rainbow" which he masturbated to, and "The Shining" contained a sense of realism that excited him.

The weeks after he returned, he struggled with his thoughts and had trouble adjusting. Girls didn't look the same anymore. Ann *Mother* confused him. He was excited about the exploration and continued to envision the girl on top of him—Ann at her side. They gave him the gift to see girls for what they were and how they made him feel: the release. The invigorating power—lifeblood—that jumpstarted the dead battery inside him.

One day, he cornered a girl in his class. He told her she looked sexy, and touched her breast. She looked scared and asked him to stop.

He did.

He never talked to her again.

Every day he tried to conceal his erection and his hunger. He was always hungry and it hurt. The more time that passed, the more the pain consumed him.

Melissa entered his life at the right moment and cultivated him. She was sixteen, an older student, but slow on the academic scale. His professor asked if he would tutor her. Surprised by the request, he accepted.

That evening she strutted into the library. Her blonde hair feathered out and blue eyeshadow covered her lids.

"So dip-shit, how did you get suckered into this?"

"What?"

"Never mind Geek-squad," she said.

"I'm Tim." He stuck out his hand and he watched in delight as she licked her palm and slid it into his.

"Melissa...Small fry"

"It's my pleasure," he said. He opened the calculus textbook and she closed it.

"Listen Shit-face, I like you. You're cute. But forget the books. Not my thing. You got a smoke?"

"What? No," he said.

"Yeah, you look like a goody two-shoes. You a virgin?"

"No."

"Bullshit. No way your got you dinky stinky geek-boy."

"I'm not a virgin. Why, are you?"

She licked her lips and with the tip of her finger touched her mouth. He gawked as she slid her finger down her neck and in between her small breasts.

"What do you think?" she asked.

He said nothing. Instead, he pushed his waistband over top of his erection.

After that day, she took him under her wing and taught him everything her mother had passed down to her. Melissa shared with him all the dirty secrets about girls' insecurities, about push buttons, and the Cat and Mouse game. She taught him the art of sex. The acts of pleasure. All the special places girls liked to be touched. He found it all intriguing. She told him she learned everything by watching her mother.

Melissa's divorced mother treated marriage as a business and she was the Donald Trump of the industry. She had four ex-husbands and she was only in her early forties.

Knowing the buttons to push to make certain girls do things—anything. She told him that not all girls could be manipulated, like boys; you had to find the right ones.

She also told him that if he ever told anyone about their special relationship that she would deny it. If he could keep his mouth shut, they could play until she finished school—two more years.

He did keep his mouth shut during the two years. He learned the craft and he was discrete. No one knew about the two.

Melissa was like him. She thought like him. She was angry like him. He didn't mind her anger. In fact, he fed off of it.

The month before Melissa's graduation, they sat together on her bed. She inhaled the bottle toke and started brewing him another. She dropped the small piece of hash on the end of the cigarette and slid it into the hole in the beer bottle. The whirl of thick smoke filled the brown bottle. She passed him the open end, removed her thumb, and with one deep breath he took it all in.

"The fucking cunt cancelled my credit card," she said.

"Why?" he said as he coughed.

"She's a bitch, that's why. 'Money's tight' she said which is bullshit. She's fucking getting ready for husband number five and needs to buy a new dress."

"You could always kill her and collect on the insurance."

He laughed.

She didn't.

The next week she revealed what she was thinking of doing and asked him if he would help. He told her he would.

Tim did most of the forensic research. He read every book in the school's library on police procedures, focusing on crime scene and evidence collection. His knowledge grew and so did his excitement. The thought of murder fascinated him and he knew he was smart enough to get away with it. Melissa was happy with the plan he suggested and she pleasured him for it.

Wednesday night, her mother arrived home at nine after a date with her, soon to be bereaved, fiancée. Her long blonde feathered hair that matched Melissa's, was a thick mane that hung down past her shoulders.

Melissa moved in fast with the crowbar high above her head. She held the bar with two hands and brought it down hard, as her mother turned toward her. The first blow opened a cut on her mother's forehead. Tim was surprised by the lack of blood.

Her mother's eyes closed as the second blow opened up a gusher. The blood sprayed in a sheet of red mist. Thick crimson fluid followed and the cast-off from the bar lined the white ceiling. The blood pattern looked similar to the picture in the book.

The woman didn't scream but Melissa did and the scream rung in his ears. His hard cock vibrated in his jeans. His blood burned hot.

She dropped the crowbar and Tim moved around and faced her. He stepped over top of the mother lying on the ceramic tiled floor. He noticed a chunk of skin that hung from the side of her head as the blood pooled beneath her. Melissa was heaving, her chest lifted in rapid succession, and he could tell from her face that she was exhausted.

He wasn't sure if he was going to go through with it. *Too late.* He raised the knife from behind his back and slammed it into her chest right where he thought her heart would be. The knife drove in so deep that the handle's edge embedded into the wound.

The look in her eyes enthralled him-pure shock. It was incredible. The warm blood ran down his arm and soaked his sleeve. He pulled the knife from her chest. It made a sucking noise. He held her by her shoulder and he could hear squishing and sucking sounds as he stuck her eleven more times.

Melissa's face lost all color as her spirit left her body.

Later, in the forest, he stood naked among the trees as he burned his clothes. Although it was cold outside, he felt hot. He felt electric. He scrubbed the blood from his body. He scrubbed so hard his skin stung with redness.

No one would ever know what he did. *How could they? He was smart. He left no trace of himself behind.* Not one person knew of their relationship. It was a secret. He scrubbed.

***

The towel on the floor soaked up all the water from the mess he made. The floor was dry. The floor was clean. He handed Christine the wet towel and she took it back to the kitchen. The fireplace flickered and the heat warmed him.

"What am I going to do with you?" she said as she returned.

"What do you want to do?"

She sat down beside him and kissed his cheek.

"Tim, you're a dog. But, I like you. I might just put a collar on you."

She kissed him, this time on the mouth.

That day she looked after him. Like a mother would. She looked so much like Ann: such an uncanny resemblance. Yet, she was nothing like *her*. She made him feel different and for the first time since Melissa, he let the thought of a relationship enter into his mind. *Crazy.*

TWENTY-SEVEN

Back in Manhattan, Christine was drinking her second cup of coffee and the morning was dragging on. She was feeling jittery from the caffeine and she was thinking about the incredible weekend she spent with Tim.

Jefferies walked passed her desk and interrupted her thoughts. He looked like he hadn't showered in weeks and the beard on his face was a reflection of how he must have spent his weekend. Christine placed her purse down in the bottom drawer and went over to his desk.

"So what's with you? You going for the George Michael look?"

"Ha-ha. Very fucking funny," he said.

"Whoa, what's your problem?"

"Oh, don't you start too."

"No really, what's going on?"

"She left. Teresa up and left. She took Sarah with her."

"I'm so sorry. What happened?"

"Big fight on Friday night. I think we're done."

She placed her arm on his shoulder and he pushed it away. The action was not like him. He was rattled.

"Don't."

"Ok. I just want to make sure you're ok."

"I'm fine. Can we change the subject?"

"Alright. You talk with Crystal about the rape case?" she said.

"Not yet. I was waiting for you."

"No time like the present," she said.

A few minutes later, the detectives joined Crystal in the lab. The room was dark and Crystal was shining a blue light over a pair of jeans.

"It's my two favorite detectives. What's with you Jefferies, did you lose your razor?" Crystal said.

"What's with everyone today? Drop it," Jeffries said.

"Jeffries and I are on the Tina Russo case."

"Hey I heard. So I guess you need updates."

Christine heard Jefferies grumble under his breath as Crystal moved toward the front of the lab and flipped a switch. Christine had to wait for her eyes to adjust to the change in lighting before she could focus on Crystal.

"I have to tell you we don't have much to go on. I examined the crime scene and found no trace evidence that would link anyone to the murder. No hair or fingerprints. Except for the victim and the father. The room was wiped clean. Just a lot of blood from the twelve stab wounds. That's why I have it on the back burner."

"You're kidding?"

"No. Sorry."

"What do you have?" Christine asked.

"The killer must have used a condom because we didn't find any semen. She was definitely raped though. The ME found vaginal bruising."

"What about witnesses. Did any of her neighbors hear or see anything?"

"Nope. Can't help you there. All dead ends."

"Do you have any good news?" Jeffries asked.

"With Tina, nothing. But we may have another homicide that matches the same MO."

"Why do you say that?" Christine asked.

"The ME has the body. We haven't discovered the identity yet, but we know that she was raped and she was stabbed twelve times. Just like Tina," Crystal said.

"Is that all there is to tie the two cases together?"

"Both victims had ligature marks on their extremities. It's not a solid link but it's something to work on."

What the hell was happening? Were people going mad? The city was in chaos; serial killers were becoming a trend. She blamed the show "Dexter" for that. She reached for something that would ground her and she thought of Tim.

"So when are you going down to the ME's?"

"She said she would be done examining the body by 11:30."

"It's 9:30 now, so let's meet at the MEs office just after eleven. Jeffries, wanna grab a coffee and get out of the office for a bit?"

"Sure," he said.

Outside, Twenty-First Street was quiet as she walked down the sidewalk. Jeffries moved along the line of police vehicles, touching them with his fingers as he passed leaving streaks behind in the dirt. As she passed the trees memories of the past weekend flooded in. Christine took in enough air to fill her lungs. It wasn't the fresh forest air of the Catskills—not fresh at all— polluted and thick.

She would try this time. She would let him inside. She needed to. She had to. The idea of going through life alone scared the shit out of her.

She crossed the street and entered Gramercy Park. The only personal sanctuary close to the precinct and the place where she liked to go to think. The park was an oasis in a small section of Manhattan and it took up a whole block between Twenty-first and Twentieth.

"So what are you going to do?" she asked.

"About what?"

"Stop with the bullshit. What are you going to do about Teresa?"

"Fucked if I know."

She moved ahead of him and sat on a bench in the middle of the park. The wood was cold but her coat padded the space between the bench and her. Jeffries sat beside her, pulled out a cigarette, and lit it.

The concrete skyscrapers sheltered them but the air snuck through and chilled her.

"What did she say?"

"She's pissed, Christine, and I don't understand one bit of it. I provide for the family. I work my ass off for the city, and what do I get from her? Nothing but flack. What the fuck am I supposed to do?"

He took another drag and exhaled the smoke increasing the pollution ever so slightly. She placed her hand on his arm and gave it a squeeze.

"It's simple. We're not that complicated."

"What do you mean?"

"Are you dense? Women. All we want is a little communication. We want to feel like we're being heard. We want to feel appreciated. So think about it. Do you do that?"

"Who has time for all that shit? By the time I get home, I'm fucking exhausted. The last thing I want to do is chat it up."

"Man, you're helpless," she said.

The wind picked up. She shivered as it crept down the back of her coat, and lowered her core body temperature. The sun reflected off the windows of the cars that drove down Twenty-First Street.

"It's cold today," she said.

"Yep."

TWENTY-EIGHT

Tim paced inside his condominium, through the living room, and into the kitchen. He snatched the blue bottle from the shelf and whipped it against the wall. The bottle shattered and the debris littered the wood floor. He fell back onto the counter as tears wet his eyes. He fought the demons raging inside him and they were winning. Just minutes before he had gathered all the mementos that he collected from each of the victims and stuffed them away in the garbage bag clutched in his hand.

As he moved through his apartment gathering the items all he could picture was the terror in his victims eyes—the blood. It felt as if he was driving at mach speed and the light turned red. Everything came to sudden halt and he shook from the mental impact. Now he crouched on the floor waiting to make his move. He wanted more. He had planned all aspects of his life since the age of twelve. From the moment he killed Melissa, and up to this point, he thought that he would live like the phoenix and burn. Christine was the stop sign. *What was it about her? Why was she so good to him?* He looked at the shards of glass on the floor. The reminder of what he is. What he has become—a killer. *No!*

He slid along the floor and brushed the glass into a pile. A sharp piece cut into the flesh of his palm, tearing open a line in his skin.

Blood streaked the floor as he swept the remnants of the broken pieces and tossed them into the bag. The last piece of the evidence that linked him to the crimes all collected at the bottom of the green plastic garbage bag.

He hoisted himself up off the cold floor and turned on the tap. Blood droplets splashed onto the gunmetal sink and washed down the drain. He wrapped the dishtowel around his hand and squeezed until the flow stopped and his knuckles turned to the same shade of white that circled the sun.

Off again. Toting the garbage bag out the front door and down to the chute. The souvenirs of the victims fell down to the container below mixing with hundreds of bags never to be seen again.

He had made his decision and now would have to conjure a way to cope with his hunger. To dull the drive he felt every minute of every day.

Back inside his condominium, he placed a band-aid on the open wound. He conquered the demons for now and he felt victorious. Unlike the control he subjected on others, controlling himself left him somewhat harmonious with the world around him. It was difficult to quiet the demons. The pain he felt was so vivid he could taste it, and that made it that much sweeter.

He thought of Christine, her soft eyes. Her face reminded him of biting into a crisp sweet melon as it crunched between his teeth as the juices exploded over his taste buds. It felt tranquil like the absorption of cannabis into the blood stream. He had the immediate desire to see her face.

He palmed the holster clipped to his belt, and with his thumb and index finger pulled out his Blackberry. He forgot the recent self-infliction he incurred and the pain shot up his arm the instant the Blackberry pressed into the wound. He rolled the dial to find Christine's name in the contacts-folder and pressed send. The black clock on the wall in the kitchen ticked. It read 11:30am.

The knock on the door slammed him out his thoughts and he ended the call. It came again, this time with a sense of urgency. He marched from the kitchen, passed the living room, and stopped at the door. He opened it just as another knock pounded out.

Simone stood in the doorframe with a dogmatic gesture. She was wearing a black leather jacket. Her milky face flashed white-hot with anger. Lines formed between her eyes as she peered into his.

"Where the fuck have you been?" she asked.

He stood there, silent and dormant. *How the hell did she know where I lived?* He shook his head. *Nope, still there.*

"Well? Didn't you get my messages?"

This enraged him and he felt claustrophobic. Simone had broken one of his rules and intruded into his private space. The principle Melissa taught him—never bring the mouse to the back door—yet here she stood. Deal with this.

He pulled her into his apartment, out of earshot of his neighbors, and closed the door. He shoved her and she slipped on the rug. She braced herself against the wall to stop the momentum that would have ended with her sprawled out on the floor.

"What are you doing here?"

"Huh?"

"You heard me. How did you find out where I lived?"

"What's your problem?"

"Fucking answer me!"

She backed away and scurried into the living room.

"I'm not liking your tone," she said.

There was a change in her voice and a level of confidence he hadn't noticed before.

"You can't just do what you did and not call me. It's not like you just fucked me or something. We killed someone."

He was becoming unglued and before he knew what he was doing, his hands were around her throat. He could feel his arm shake as he squeezed the life from her. Her knees gave out and she fell to the sofa. He moved along with her applying more pressure as he did so. Her eyes were frantic and shifted wildly. His hip vibrated from the ringing Blackberry. He squeezed harder. It vibrated again and he remembered that he just dialed Christine. The thought of her as his hands wrapped around Simone's throat made his head swim. He felt it first in his stomach, and then in his throat. Hot fluid rushed out his mouth and out his nostrils. His vomit splashed over the white sofa. He released his grip and Simone sucked in air. The breath was loud and she was coughing.

She skittered away from him and heaved again.

"You stay away from me. Fucking stay away from me!"

He sat down on the coffee table. *What was that?*

His head floated on his neck and it felt heavy as he searched for understanding. He came up empty. Simone was huddled in the corner between the sofa and steel, floor lamp. She looked terrified. Like a battered animal. Her eyes fluttered with a panicked expression. He felt sick again but he swallowed it back.

"I'm sorry Simone."

"Sorry? If you ever touch me like that again I'll cut your nuts off."

"What do you want?"

"I missed you," she said.

"You're fucked,"

"What's that supposed to mean?"

"Think about it Simone. Last week you and I raped and murdered a woman. Just now, I almost killed you. And you miss me?"

"So. It's not like that was my idea. It was yours. And yes, I do."

"Forget it. It was fun while it lasted but now I'm sorry to say it's over. In fact, after today, it's best that we don't see each other again"

Her face shot back a stung expression from the statement. As the shock wore off her facial features morphed. She looked ugly. Angry.

"No. No. No. No. No...No!"

"Simone, calm down."

"No way Tim. You're not dumping me. No fucking way."

"I have to go to work. You have to leave. We'll talk about this later. Ok?"

The phone continued to vibrate as he ushered Simone out the door.

TWENTY-NINE

Christine was accustomed to looking at dead bodies and the body of the Jane Doe in front of her was no different; but the smell was like a punch to the gut. It knocked the wind out of her every time.

The Y-shaped cut pattern across the victim's chest was fresh and the stapled sutures reminded her of train tracks. Lights from above showered the room with white, which uncovered too much detail for Christine to tolerate in one solitary glance.

"Most likely the death was pericardial effusion. This caused cardiac tamponade..."

"Doc, in English please?" Christine asked.

"Basically, internal bleeding from the twelve stab wounds filled the victim's chest and blocked the heart's ventricles from filling properly. This was the cause of death."

"Is that what's going into the report?" Jeffries asked.

"Yes and that's my final answer Regis," the ME said.

"That's not funny." Christine said.

"Anyway, I found some skin under her fingernails." The ME handed Crystal a plastic jar.

"Look here." She pointed to Christine and leaned over the steel table. The ME was using stainless steel tongs to point to the labia.

"There was extreme bruising and tearing both inside and outside. Do you see that?"

Looking at a dead woman's vagina was morbid and disturbing. She saw the tear. It was slight but it was there on the right lip. The bruising was harder to make out, but after moving in closer, the discoloration became apparent.

"From what I can tell a foreign object was used to penetrate the victim."

"What are saying?" Jeffries said.

"I think she means a dildo. Is that right?" Crystal said.

"That is exactly what I was saying."

"Ok, so I'm a little confused here, Doc. Are saying a woman did this?"

"You're the detective I just give you the facts. Whether a man or a woman did this is undetermined. I can't rule out either sex at this point."

Christine watched as Crystal removed the camera lens and proceeded to snap photos of the victim. Christine backed away. Jeffries seemed to be lost in thought. The bearded look was starting to grow on her.

"Crystal, make sure you get shots of the ligature marks. I want you to compare that to the marks found on Tina."

"No problem. I'll find you as soon as I have some results," Crystal said.

"What's next?" Jeffries asked.

"I guess we give the picture to the media and hope someone recognizes her photo. We should probably canvas the neighborhood where they found the body."

"I'm glad I wore my comfortable shoes today," Jeffries said.

She thought of the hike on the weekend. Her thighs still burned. She wasn't looking forward to pounding the sidewalks.

The Ritz would be the last stop and it was four blocks from the alley where they found the body. Christine's heels clicked on the marble floors. Gold etching lined the ceiling and a chandelier hung in the middle half way down the lobby. The lounge was off to the right and it was filled with afternoon patrons. She noticed a full table of women sitting together on the wall closest to her. A woman with straight blonde hair caught her eye and stared back at her as she walked past. She wore a stylish dress and the woman's fur coat was draped across the back of her chair. The look made Christine feel cheap and outclassed.

Ahead, behind the desk, the hotel clerk finished with his customer. He smiled warmly at Christine and her partner.

"Welcome to the Ritz Carleton. How may I help you?"

She flashed her badge and placed the photo of the Jane Doe on the counter.

"I need you to look at this photo and tell me if you recognize this woman."

The image was touched up but she was sure by the disgusted expression on his face that he knew he was looking at a corpse.

"Sorry. I can't say I have. You might want to check with the bartender in there. He sees most of the action around this place."

"Thanks," she said.

She passed the blonde haired woman as she entered the lounge. This time their eyes avoided confrontation. The bartender slipped a martini glass on the bar as Christine waved him over. He stuck up his index finger as if to say *just a minute.* She waved back her badge and he stopped pouring a beer.

"What can I do for you?" he said as he slid his hand along the bar.

"Can you take a look at a photo and tell me if you recognize her."

"Sure thing," he said.

He took the photo from Christine and studied it like it was a rare artifact.

"Well?" Jeffries asked.

"Hold on a sec. I'm looking. You know what... I think I've seen her before."

"Seriously?" Christine said.

"I'm certain of it. She was here last week. You couldn't forget her. She was the type of woman that could convert a priest. If you know what I mean."

He winked at Jeffries. Christine was not impressed.

"Ok, so she was attractive. Can you tell us anything else?"

"Yep, she was with another couple. A redhead that looked good but not as hot as the Asian did though. The guy I can't tell you too much. I didn't really look at him you know."

"Do you mind coming down to the station and working with our sketch artist?"

"No problem."

"Ok, great. Listen we're going to need to talk to the hotel manager. Can you page him or her for us?"

"Done."

The bartender moved down to the opposite end of the bar and picked up the house phone. A man beside the women drinking the Martini stared at the half empty beer glass under the tap. He looked anxious. *Poor guy.*

After speaking with the manager, they found out that a guest last week removed linen from one of the suites. The house cleaner also found it odd that the room was spotless. Too clean. The room was registered under the name Simone Adams.

THIRTY

Tim entered Stone Temple Pilots into the touch screen remote. The screen flashed a list of albums, he chose "Thank you", and the Mark Levinson speakers woke from their slumber and pounded out the song "Vaseline". The window cooled his hands as he leaned into it. A sea of concrete littered the landscape below. Tall buildings flowed down the horizon as far as his eyes could see. He could smell the city and it seemed to breathe. He closed his eyes and pictured a sea of green covering the concrete outside as if grass and dirt had dropped from the heavens, blanketing the city streets; the buildings changed into majestic mountains: a place where he could inhale air and not consume a mouthful of exhaust fumes.

Simone's unwarranted visit violated his plans for the day. In one instant, she changed everything and left Tim unhinged. His hip vibrated. He completely forgot about Christine's call. He looked at the time. It was 6:15pm.

"Hello," he said.

"Hey, what happened to you? You called me and hung up. Is everything ok?"

"Christine, I'm so sorry. A friend of mine knocked on my door as I was dialing your number. He stayed for a while and I lost track of time."

"Ok."

Christine's voice whispered through the receiver, and at once, he clicked into gear. He had her laughing as he described his amusing friend. He told her a fictitious story that he pasted together from fabricated images that appeared like apparitions from the darkness of his mind.

"Enough already, you're killing me. So, what's up?" she said.

"I wanted to get together for dinner."

"We made a break in the murder case I told you about. So I don't think I can. We can meet at my place for a drink later though."

"Oh. Are you close by? Maybe we can grab a coffee."

"No sorry I'm near the Ritz. I have to go back to the precinct now, but after seven, I'll be uptown. So if you want we can grab a quick one, but I'd rather just meet up after my shift."

As she said the words, neurons fired, and his mind raced with concern. He pieced together the Ritz, the case, and uptown. Simone lived in uptown. He wondered what possible evidence he or Simone left behind. He always made it part of the protocol to be meticulous.

"No you're right, we should get together after. I guess I'm just anxious to see you."

He assessed all the possible outcomes and the ramifications of what would happen if they interviewed Simone. None were positive.

"I was hoping we could get together too. Miss you Baby," she said.

"Ok. See you tonight."

After the call ended, he immediately dialed Simone's number.

Simone sat on the bed. Her body language revealed the confusion she must have felt. He liked that she wore her emotions like the front cover of a fiction novel; this allowed him to profile her every move. Tim handed her the stainless steel revolver and the weight of the weapon must have surprised her, because her arm fell to her lap.

"It's heavy," she said.

"I know."

"Is it loaded?"

"Of course. The safety's on. Either way, be careful."

"I've never used a gun before."

"Don't worry, it's easy. Just point and squeeze the trigger," he said.

She moved the gun from her lap and pointed it toward the bedroom closet. He placed his hand on the top of the gun and removed the weapon from her hands with a handkerchief.

"What are doing?" she said.

"Getting rid of the prints," he wiped the gun clean removing his prints and placed the revolver on Simone's bureau. His image reflected back in the mirror. He liked how his face looked: the high cheekbones and his chiseled jaw. He has been told he looks like Guy Pierce, but Tim thought he had one up on Guy because of his blue-grey eyes.

"Why don't we just run away together? You have the money," she said.

"It's not possible, not with those two detectives chasing you. There is only one solution. You need to kill them."

"What if I can't?"

"Don't talk like that," he said. He slipped his hand down the curve of her back and held her. He patted her thigh and kissed the side of her neck. She gasped and pulled him into a tight embrace.

"You have the element of surprise. They won't see it coming. Trust me," he said.

"Ok. Then we can be together," she said.

"Yes, Simone, forever."

He explained the remaining details of the plan and left her alone in her apartment to stew on her emotions.

He exited her building through the garage. The air seemed less polluted today and actually somewhat fresh.

Up above, he noticed a large black bird perched on the lamppost outside. The bird's feathers gleamed from the blazing red sun and the crow radiated black-red. It made him think of the phoenix rising from the ashes: reborn. He smiled wide, exposing his white teeth to the bird. It held his stare and Tim was sure the bird nodded. He checked his watch and it was 6:59pm. *Perfect.* The day had moved along with velocity and he had forgotten to take the time to nourish his muscles: his gut reminded him as it growled.

He walked up Columbus Avenue passing little shops carved into an old red brick building. Above, fire escapes lined the outside; climbing like snakes to the top floors.

The wind picked up, whistled through his hair, and tickled his ear. He pulled his black coat tight around his chest and increased his pace.

Graffiti plastered a white delivery truck just outside Lenny's bar. He stopped to glance through the open window. A group of four men sat at the back of the bar and other than them, the place was empty. He swept the front door open and a rush of air soaked him with heat. Stale beer and fry grease filled his nostrils—not his first choice—but it would have to do.

As he sat near the window, he calculated tonight's outcome. Someone would die, he was certain of that but Christine stood the best chance. She had the advantage of police training and she had a partner. Still nothing in life was ever certain.

THIRTY-ONE

The soft hum died as Christine turned off the ignition. She parked out front of Simone Adam's building. Parked cars lined both sides of 74th Street and a brown awning hung above the entrance to her apartment building.

"This is it," she pointed to the doors.

Inside, she showed the guard her credentials. He scanned her I.D as if he was eyeing a cheeseburger, and she tapped her foot in response.

"It look's legit. The elevator is around the corner on the right. Is she in any trouble?"

Jeffries turned his nose down to the guard, "You're kidding right," Jeffries said.

The detectives passed the guard leaving him to consume his black coffee and the half-eaten sandwich that littered his desk.

In the elevator, Christine pressed the button that engaged the machine above to take them to the seventh floor.

"So what do you think?" Jefferies asked.

"I think it's great to see you without that beard on your face."

"What do you mean?"

"You know what I mean. You were on your way down. Once we close the case, you need to take some time off and go get your wife back. That's what I think."

"I really messed it up, didn't I?"

"If you don't get some counseling you're going to lose your family. I mean it. Once this is closed…"

"Yeah…yeah. I know," he said.

She would use some of her own advice; as soon as this was finished, she would focus on her new relationship. After the interview, she would close it down for the day and get ready for Tim. His face was the first one she wanted to see when this was all over. She would tell him that they have a reason to celebrate. Any reason to see him would be fine with her.

Outside apartment 705, Christine knocked on the door.

She waited.

Knocked again.

Then she heard movement on the other side of the door. The eyehole flashed.

"NYPD Miss. Adams. We need to speak to you. Open the door please," she said.

The detectives looked at each other and shook their heads in amazement, at the closed door.

"Somebody is in there," Jefferies said.

Christine banged on the door.

Nothing.

She heard a familiar clicking sound, followed by an explosion of wood. The splinters scratched at her cheek. She reached down, pulled out the police issue Glock, crouched while moving back from the door, and placed the gun in position. Another shot fired through the door and beams of light pushed out from the two bullets holes. Dust floated in the air in the tubes of white light.

Jefferies backed up against the far wall and away from the gunfire. Christine pulled out her blackberry called in the code for a 10-32.

With backup on the way, she motioned to Jefferies to kick down the door. The first kick bent the doorframe. The second slammed the door into the apartment. She went in low and she felt Jefferies behind her, his gun pointing out beside her.

They swept fast. First through the kitchen, then the living room, and the bathroom. All clear. The bedroom door was closed. Jefferies turned the door handle and pushed the door open. Another bullet sailed past him shattering a picture on the wall.

"Drop the gun Simone! No one needs to get hurt," Christine said.

Christine cornered the doorframe, turning away quickly as another bullet almost ended her life.

Her heart raced and she whispered to Jefferies that Simone was behind the bed. Christine motioned for him to cover her. He did. She sidled into the doorway and fired two quick shots.

One hit the woman in the chest between her breasts and the other landed about an inch below the first. Simone fell back against the window and the gun in her hand dropped to the floor. Simone followed, her body slid down the wall, landing hard on the floor, and slumped against the bed.

Sitting alone in the quiet room at the precinct, she felt at odds with the day's events. It left her in a state of shock. This was her first kill and whether in self-defense or not, was the part of the job that she worried about. She tried her best to avoid pulling the trigger. She had had no choice.

The steel chair hurt her back and she shifted to try to get comfortable but it was no use. The room was painted a soft grey. They say that grey seemed to soothe your senses, and calm your nerves in stressful situations. Calm was not an emotion she could conjure. She had never been through this before. She had fired her weapon three other times since she had started with the force. None had ended with a fatality. In either case, the procedure was the same. Department policy spelled out that she would be off duty for a week; until internal affairs confirms that it was good shoot.

The union rep arrived. He confirmed what she already knew, one week paid administrative leave. He reassured her that this was not a suspension and the leave did not imply that she did anything wrong. *No kidding! But that didn't change the fact that she took someone's life today.*

The meeting ended and she headed straight for the Captain's office, leaving behind the dreary soft grey room. Jefferies was already in the office, sitting in the chair to her right.

"I've read Jefferies report, everything looks clean and by the book," said the Captain.

She said nothing. She tried to make eye contact with him but all she could picture was the bullets striking Simone.

"Yes sir, like I wrote in my report it was a clean shoot. There was no other option. The suspect fired four shots. There was no communication on her side. Christine yelled to the suspect to drop the gun. She looked straight at me and aimed the gun right at my chest. If Christine didn't take the shot I wouldn't be sitting here right now to tell you about it."

"So, what you're saying in this report is that Simone Adams killed both Tina Russo and the Jane Doe. Is that correct?"

"It would seem to point that way," she said.

"Christine, you have some reservations?"

"Captain, all the evidence points to Simone Adams." Jefferies said.

"Ok, so nothing is going to come back and bite us in the ass?"

"Nothing," said Jefferies.

"Ok, so is there anything else you want to add to this Christine?" asked the Captain.

She said nothing.

"Good, the press has been all over me to make a statement," said the Captain.

The captain had already changed into his dress blues and had his game face on. Christine hated politics and could care less about being anything more than a Detective.

"Ok Detectives, that is all. Christine, I will see you back here in a week."

Christine met with a representative from I.A after the meeting with the captain. Christine explained the details of the events that led up to the shooting and after she answered a few of his questions, he told her that she could go.

THIRTY-TWO

Tim flipped through Christine's family photo album while she used the washroom. The album cover felt rough in his palm and the book had a worn look to it, as if it had been read over a thousand times. The pages hung to the bindings by threads. The pictures were beautiful. Memories of how a family should be. He looked at a photo of Christine, as a child. She held an unwrapped present in her hands and she was brimming from ear to ear with enthusiasm. Her father must have taken the picture because both her sister and her mother sat on the sofa next to the tree.

"Hey. Whatcha lookin' at?" she asked as he watched her approach from the bathroom.

"You were so absolutely adorable."

"Thank you."

"What was the present?" He showed her the photo and her eyes lit-up; and they looked almost as they did back then.

"Oh my God! I remember that. It was the first Christmas in our new house. Dad was promoted to detective that year. It was a copy of "The Kachina Doll Mystery" a detective story for kids and a pair of fake handcuffs. Believe it or not, that was my favorite present that I ever got."

"For some reason, I don't have a hard time with that," he said. He closed the photo album and placed it on the coffee table. He felt jealous of Christine and of her family but held that in, camouflaging his emotions like a wooden stick-bug blending in among the forest's trees.

She reached up to him and he noticed tears were streaming down her face. She kissed his mouth. It tasted salty from her tears. He liked it: a familiar flavor.

"You ok?" he asked.

"A little better, I've never killed anyone before," she said.

He almost let—*you'll get over it*—slip out. Instead, he blocked the words before they could pass from his mind to his lips.

"I'm sorry you're going through this."

"The worst thing is that I have to sit here in my apartment for a week and play the images over and over again in my mind."

"Can you leave the city?" he said. He thought of the Caves and wondered if you could get a reservation with this short notice.

"Of course, why?" she said.

"You got a computer with an internet connection?"

"Sure, my laptop's in the bedroom and I have Wi-Fi but are you going to tell me anything, or are you going to keep asking me questions? I feel like you're the cop. Sheesh."

"Just go get it and I'll show you. Trust me."

With the laptop fired up, Tim typed the resorts website into the internet web browser. He watched as the page loaded. A flash photo program started and a slide show of the resorts images lit up the screen, as well as Christine's eyes. Waves crashed into a cliff at the edge of the resort. Small huts carved into the rock and lush palms scattered across the cliffs. He clicked on the reservations button and another screen with a calendar popped up. He entered in the date he wanted.

"Looks like I can get us in for Wednesday through Saturday. You in?"

"Tim, the resort looks great. It looks like they built it on top of a cliff. How much is it?"

"I'll take that as a yes," he said.

"I said, how much, not yes."

"Don't worry about the cost. I'll arrange everything. My treat."

Her eyes moved back to the screen and she was lost in the resort's photos.

"Really, can we even get a flight?"

"Again, leave that to me."

She closed the laptop and placed it on the coffee table beside the dilapidated photo album, turned toward him and placed her hand in his. Her hand felt rough, not soft, like his. And her fingernails could use some attention, but her arms had lots of definition. She was beautiful and she reminded him of Mariska Hargitay. He pulled her up off of the couch and walked her to the bedroom.

On the bed, he held her against his chest and her heart thumped in hers. Her perfume had a zing of citrus and he could smell tangerine and blackcurrant. It was exquisite and glamorous and not what he expected.

"Is this a new perfume?"

"You like it?" she asked.

"Definitely." He kissed the side of her neck and she curled up like an armadillo under attack. She pulled her knees up and squealed as he kissed her again. Wrapping his arms tighter around her, he cuddled into her from behind and she felt good in his arms.

"Tim, you're the best," she said.

"If I didn't know any better I would think your coming on to me." He turned her over so they met face to face and gave her a couple of baby kisses.

"I really like you," she said and she returned his soft kisses.

He brushed her cheek with the back of his hands and wiped away the stray hairs that fell on her face. Looking into her eyes was like watching a good movie. He felt lost in them. No matter how long he stared, her eyes seemed to go on forever: they were deep green and lush, like a rain forest. Her skin melted together in a complexion of olive and bronze.

"What are you thinkin?" she asked.

"About you."

"Oh yeah."

"Yeah," he said.

Ten minutes later, Christine was fast asleep. Her chest rose and fell in small waves. He remembered looking at Christine's photo album and a sea of emotions drowned him in deep reflections. He thought about his life as a child and wondered if things would have turned out differently if his father never died or if Ann acted more like a mother than that of a monster.

Tim was in his last year of university at MIT. He crossed over Harvard Bridge, down Massachusetts Avenue, and entered the on ramp to I90 west. During rush hour traffic, the highway would be jammed but Tim left after the blitz and the roads were open. He followed the speed limit, avoiding a confrontation with highway patrol, and a possible speeding ticket that could be traced back to him, contradicting his alibi.

He had left his car parked in the clear view of the university's security cameras. Today he drove Sandy's car.

He met Sandy during his first year at MIT. She was studying computer science. She had an odd way about her and that was one of the attractions. He took her by force just like the others.

He controlled her just like he mastered the guitar. It was difficult at first but with constant repetition and guidance, she conformed.

Two weeks ago, he received an unexpected and unwanted visit from Berta. She revealed to him what she had witnessed working for his mother. About the horrors that he suffered during her tenure. She wanted him to know that she cared for him too late and that she was sorry that she stood by and let his mother abuse him.

None of her condolences intrigued him but the news she alleged about his Father's death enraged him. She disclosed his mother's filthy secret—that Ann killed his father—something his mother confessed to Berta during an alcohol-fueled argument. Her exact words were "I'll kill you like I killed my husband". Ann had been drinking excessively and hadn't remembered the exchange the next day, but Berta did and handed in her resignation that morning.

He followed I95 south for three hours until the Manhattan skyline breached the horizon. He continued onto Hwy 695 toward the Hamptons.

He started planning the day Berta left and two weeks later, he was now ready to execute it.

He arrived at the house at 10:30pm. The light from the sun had long expired and darkness fell on the green grass changing it to ash grey. With Berta gone, Ann would be alone in the house. That he hoped. If he stumbled upon an unexpected guest, well that would be unfortunate and they would be snuffed out. *No remorse.*

He moved across the backyard as the light from the moon uncovered shadows among the trees and dark fingers scraped over the bark. He thought of demons, the kind that devoured souls of the departed and he didn't fear them: he walked among them, sharing their essence.

He could see her in the window. She sat on a new blue striped sofa. She looked aged. Hard.

He reached the side door opposite the pool. The side entrance led to the ground floor laundry room. With a flick of the knife's handle, the glass cracked, and the frosted pieces fell to the floor. The distance from the laundry room to the living room, where Ann was sitting, was far enough away that the sounds the glass made as it shattered on the ceramic tile would fall only on his ears.

He waited for the alarm to sound. As he expected, Ann had sent away the only person that knew how to program the alarm and a smile crept across his face.

He left the shards of glass on the floor and took the back stairs up to the master bedroom.

He waited in the bathroom amongst the sea of white porcelain. Soon. His heart ran at a smooth rate as he breathed deep, calming his nerves. Tonight he wanted to experience the events with all senses firing.

Later, she slept deeply while he stood at the foot of her bed. The white comforter fell loose from her and her bare shoulder pointed up toward the ceiling. Her arms were folded across her chest and they moved slightly as she exhaled. Her raven hair fell across the pillow in streams.

Tim moved in, slipped the loop of the scarf around her ankle, and tied the other end to the bedpost below. She stirred as he smoothed his soft hand over her calf. The stubble from her unshaven leg pricked at his palm as he finished tying her free ankle to the post. His heart was beating fast and it was hard to control his enthusiasm. The pilot light inside him flared up and ignited the fires of the dark caverns of his heart. He felt electric.

The last of the scarves looped around her right wrist as her eyes opened slowly. She stirred as if coming out of hibernation, and her movements were lethargic. He watched as she attempted to pull her arms free and terror washed over her as she came to the realization that she was restrained.

"What...what the...what the." She said.

"Please be quiet Ann." He tied the loop hard enough to pinch her skin and she yelped in reaction.

"Hello, Ann. I missed you. Did you miss me?"

She said nothing for the first few seconds. Instead, just shot frantic glances around the room and tried to pull loose of the restraints.

"I know what you must be thinking. This must be some kind of a sick joke. That this can't be happening. Is that what you're thinking?"

"Tim, what are you doing? Untie me."

"Um, let me think about that. How about no. Yes, that works for me. Sorry if this is making you uncomfortable but trust me this won't take too long."

"Tim! I don't think you heard me. Fucking untie me! I mean it!"

"Ann, do you mind if I call you Mother? Yes, Mother is good. Wouldn't you say after all the years I deserve that?"

She looked back now and she was not the person he remembered. This woman tied to the bed looked fragile, small, not a woman that could have terrorized him. What reflected back from her eyes was pure unfiltered fear. He loved it. He could smell it seep from her skin. It was delicious and savory. Full of the most exquisite flavor: a juicy medium rare filet with melted garlic butter. Hmmm...

"Do you remember the night you turned me into a man? Do you remember, Mother? Please tell me you remember?"

"Tim, what do you want? Why are you doing this?"

Her voice was a mere whisper shaking ever so softly like a child's confession with his hands out, holding a broken figurine.

"I asked you a question. This time stop fucking around and answer!" He pulled the eight-inch hunting knife from the back of his pants. Her eyes widened showing more of the white surrounding her pupils.

"Ok. Ok. Ok. Just. Just wait a minute. I remember. Tim we were drunk. We didn't mean for that to happen. Please forgive me. Forgive me."

"Oh, I'm not upset. There is nothing to forgive. I actually wanted to thank you. That night you helped me understand who I am. Who I could become. I have to tell you, I'm beginning to perfect the craft."

"You're not making any sense. What are talking about?"

He held the knife with the comfort of a butcher. The knife was now a part of him: an extension of his arm. He controlled it as he would control the movement of a finger. He slipped the knife under the comforter and slid it up along the length of her leg. Her thigh flinched from the embrace of the cold steel.

"Get that fucking thing away from me."

She pulled her body away from him—at least as far as the scarves would allow. He ripped the comforter from the bed leaving her exposed. Her limbs were thicker with age and small pouch protruded from her stomach.

"Gaining a little weight, Mother. You should watch that you know. Men won't like you if you look like that. Or should I say women?"

"Fuck you!"

"Mother, I know. I know what you did. I just want to hear it come from your lips, from your mouth, and whispered through your teeth."

"What are you talking about?"

"You killed my Father. I want the confession."

"You're crazy. You're out of your mind," she said.

He leaped from the floor and onto the bed. He landed straddling her. The blade of the knife rested against the loose skin on her neck.

"You tell me. Tell me now or I'll cut your fucking throat."

He applied pressure to the handle and a trickle of blood wet the blade.

"Ok. Ok. I killed him. Is that what you want to hear? He was a waste of a man and I killed him. I unbuckled his seat belt and crashed the car into the tree. Is that what you wanted to hear? Does that make you happy? Did you get what you came for?"

He released the pressure off of the blade. He straightened his back and sat with her between his thighs. Her eyes closed and her head turned away. She looked so vulnerable—perfect.

"Mother I have only a few rules. One: you will not scream. Two: you will do what I say. Three: you will bleed."

Her eyes flashed as the last rule struck home and as squishing and sucking sounds filled the room. Blood gurgled from the wounds and sprayed up like a geyser soaking the sheets. He stuck the blade into her, not stopping until he counted the exact amount. Twelve for the day she allowed her friend to molest him. Twelve for the day he became a man.

THIRTY-THREE

Christine waited with Tim on the tarmac. The small plane shone white in the cold sun while massive jumbo jets taxied on the runway and towered over their charter. She felt a little nervous about flying but Tim was very reassuring. Now she looked up at the tube of death and knots tightened in the pit of her stomach.

"Hey you ready to board?" Tim asked.

He squeezed her hand gently and she followed him across the tarmac toward the stairs of the plane. She wanted to get this part over with; Christine could go hand to hand with some of the toughest criminals but the thought of flying at forty-five thousand feet, in that little thing, scared her shitless. With a deep breath, she climbed the stairs. *Nice ass. Looks great in jeans. Focus on the ass. Breathe and focus on the beautiful man.*

The plane touched down on the runway in Montego Bay. It bounced twice then the roar of the engines filled the cabin and the landing smoothed out as the tires gripped the pavement. Christine looked at her watch. It was 1:30 pm.

At Tim's request, she packed only carry-on luggage, which was good, because her summer collection was outdated and the last time she wore a bikini Michael Jackson launched his "Thriller" album.

"Welcome to Paradise," the guard said as he read over their documents.

Christine scanned the open airport. The luggage carousel consisted of one serpentine steel skeleton that transported traveler's luggage in a u-shaped pattern.

The vacationers lined the carrousel waiting for their luggage as Christine moved past, Tim leading. Some of the men dressed in Hawaiian-style shirts, while women wore halter-tops and summer wraps. Some ill-prepared travelers like Christine, wore jeans and t-shirts and the moisture in the air stuck to her like a second skin. She needed to change soon. It was hot.

Vacationers in the departure lounge sported terrific tans and some of the women wore tight braids in their hair. She looked up and the ceiling was covered with large bamboo fans that wafted hot air down on her.

Outside, a Jamaican man with grey hair held a sign that spelled out Tim's name. They walked up to him.

"Hi, I'm Tim."

They shook hands and the driver escorted them toward the black sedan.

"Welcome to beautiful Jamaica, Mon," the driver said in a thick voice.

Later, at the resort, they were met by the manager. He was a young white guy with blue eyes and dusty blonde hair. He spoke perfect English. "The private enclave of The Caves is a world apart," he said. "The resort offers ten hand-crafted wood and stone thatch-roofed cottages. They are interwoven between two acres of lush vegetation and cavernous cliffs, each with sea views."

Tim touched the small of her back. She felt tingles inside from the caress of his hand.

"Don't hesitate to call me if you need anything," he said as he handed Tim the room key.

They passed through the lobby and out into Villas. Tim showed her the breathtaking view from the safety of the wall at the cliffs.

"What do you think?" he asked.

"Tim, this place is incredible. How did you find it?" she said.

"I've traveled all over the Caribbean. Most Islands are beautiful and as long as you stay at a 5-Star resort you're fine, but this little gem was a tip from a friend. It blew me away the first time I came here and it never has disappointed me since. It's great, huh?"

She pulled him into her. She loved the feel of his arms and liked how hard his biceps looked in his white shirt.

She pulled up into him and kissed him. Their lips were hot and salty sweat from his upper lip fired off her taste buds.

She walked beside him down the path toward their villa. She could see into the cave below through a large opening in the rock. The water plunged down to a depth of thirty feet. She made out a tropical reef just below the water's surface.

"We'll get snorkel gear, at some point, and check that out," he said.

She looked forward to it. He then led them down a set of coral stairs that passed through sundecks and into grottoes.

"This is us," he pointed to a small white villa with a brown roof.

Christine entered the villa. The bedroom had a king-sized bed. Hand-carved masks and one-of-a-kind pieces of art from local artists lined the walls. Mosquito netting fell from the ceiling above the bed. On the foot of the bed, a collection of bags stood in a row.

"I Hope you don't mind, I ordered these for you. I hope they fit."

She reached into the brown paper bag and pulled out four bikinis. They were all different colors. The bag also contained matching wraps. She looked back at him. He was sitting in a brown wicker chair on the side of the bed. "Tim, they're beautiful."

"I hope they fit. I wasn't exactly sure about the sizes. Open the other ones," he said.

"Ok."

Christine pulled out two summer dresses and three pairs of sandals. One pair was thongs, the kind you slip on to hang out at the beach; the other two were more elegant. The last bag contained a collection of lingerie, bras, and G-strings.

"The panties and bras are optional," he said.

"Really." She smiled back at him.

Every item looked expensive. The quality of the material was like the kind she would admire at Victoria Secret. She would never spend that kind of money on herself.

"Check out the closet," he said.

She moved from the bed to the side closet and opened the slatted doors. In the closet, more summer dresses hung from hangers.

On the shelf sat two hats, one a baseball hat with a New York Yankees emblem and the other a floppy straw fedora. He pointed to the drawers in the dresser on the far wall. She opened drawer after drawer: shorts and shirts filled them.

Christine sat on the bed and tears filled her eyes. Never in her life had anyone ever treated her like this. Never in her life had she ever owned a wardrobe like this. "You're amazing."

She ran over and hugged him. "This place is incredible Tim. This is all too much." Her arms hung around his neck and she kissed his face, his ear, and his lips. "Everything is wonderful, Tim, I can't thank you enough."

"Just being with you is all the thanks I need."

He kissed her hard and pulled her off her feet into his arms.

"You must be starving. Let's make a reservation and I will show you the rest of the resort. You know, we even have a hot tub that has a window view of the ocean. The sunset is breathtaking."

"Hey, why don't you try on your stuff while I call down."

Later, after Christine put on one of the summer dresses they walked down between the villas, to the restaurant below. The open-air gazebo sat at the highest spot on the cliff.

The chef cooked them genuine Jamaican cuisine. They feasted on splendid home-style cooking that was prepared fresh for them and just one other couple.

During their dinner, they talked a lot. She told Tim funny stories about her parents. She could tell from his facial expression that the talk saddened him. They laughed together at the similarity between Christine and her father while sipping rum and cokes.

She noticed another couple eating at the table opposite theirs. They looked like they were married, not on a honeymoon. There was not enough touching and handholding.

The wife was a tall, blonde-haired woman. She had long legs and a skinny frame. Christine would never want to be that thin. The woman looked unhealthy. Her dress flowed open from the warm breeze; at times Christine caught a few glimpses of the woman's breast. The husband was a larger man. Not muscular like Tim: flabby. His belly protruded through his shirt and his buttons strained against the fabric, on the verge of popping.

Christine was startled out of her voyeuristic behavior.
"What's got you attention?"
"Do you see that couple over there?"
"Yes, what about them?"
"Well, have you noticed that the woman's dress has been blowing open? Christ, you can see her tits."
"I wasn't going to say anything."
They laughed.
"They're married. Sounds like they're on their 10-year anniversary. At least that's what I thought I heard her say," Christine said.
"Yeah I would guess they're in their early forties," he said.
"I haven't seen them touch once tonight, I hope we never get like that."
"No, I don't think that would ever happen."
They finished dinner and strolled along the painted rock pathways his arm draped over her shoulder. Her arm wrapped around the small of his back. The rocks

were painted light beige. Tim pointed to an opening up ahead.

"That's the jump hole."

The far edge was crusted with jagged volcanic rock. The small opening in the walls of the path gave way to the ledge. Below the blue ocean crashed against the cave wall. He moved in behind her and pushed her up toward the edge. The distance down to the water looked to be about twenty feet but she couldn't be certain. The tips of her sandals lipped over and for just a second she thought he was going to push her.

"You gotta be kidding! People jump through that? I'm not jumping in there!"

"Come on, you only live once."

She felt the pressure of his hands on her shoulders. His hands were warm, but soft, and she felt safe in them. Then she was moving backward into him.

"Let's go baby. You have to see the sunset from the patio."

Sitting in one of the loungers was the blonde woman from dinner, minus her husband. She was drinking a Martini. She stared directly at Tim as they moved into the shared space. Tim waved and her eyes lit up while she smiled back. Christine waved as well but the woman didn't return the gesture. *Bitch.*

Tim leaned against the wall and his white cotton shirt swayed in the breeze. She could see the small of his back. It made her heart skip.

The sun setting on the far off horizon filled the sky with orange mixed with blues, reds, and yellows that coated the canvas before her; no painting would ever capture the image, she thought.

"Tim, that is absolutely the best sunset I have ever seen."

"I'm thinking the same thing. I'm also thinking there isn't anyone else in the world I would want to share it with."

"You two are going to make me puke," said the woman.

Christine turned and shot the woman a disturbed look. "Pardon?" Christine said.

"Never mind me. Just jealous, I guess," she said.

"You want a drink?" Tim said.

Christine said, "Yes," and he left for the bar. She turned back as the waves crashed against the rock wall below. The ocean was so clear she could make out the sandy bottom.

Tim returned with two sweaty glasses. She took the one he handed her.

"Cheers, here's to having a great vacation," he said

"I'll drink to that."

They clanked their glasses and took long swallows. The rum was strong and there was more alcohol than mix.

They sat down on the loungers across from a hammock that floated between two poles. The wood gazebo surrounded them and wood slats crisscrossed the roof above. Small gardens filled with exotic plants were carved into the patio and was nice addition to all the rock.

"So where are you guys from?" The woman asked, reminding them she was still there.

"New York, and you?" said Tim.

The woman leaned into his comment and crossed her legs toward him.

"Texas, I'm Rebecca."

She floated out of the chair and glided over to Tim with an extended hand. He shook it. The handshake lasted a little too long for Christine. Her hand shot out and pulled Rebecca's hand away.

"I'm Christine."

The removal of her hand seemed to throw Rebecca, and the greeting was a mere brush as she pulled back her hand in the time it would take to bat an eyelash. Rebecca turned back to Tim. The flirting was starting to annoy Christine and there was no way in hell she was going to let this happen. *Not tonight.*

"Tim, it's been a long day. Do you want to get another drink and head back to the room?"

"Sounds like a great idea to me."

Dusk moved in as the horizon sucked the sun from the sky. The lights along the path lit the way to the bar.

"Party poopers," Rebecca yelled out to them as they walked away, drinks in their hands.

THIRTY-FOUR

They woke early the next morning. The Caribbean sun set the room ablaze with a shower of white mixed with yellow. The skin on Christine's back stuck to him from the humidity. He kissed the back of her neck.

"Morning sunshine," she said.

"Good morning baby."

They showered together and it lasted as long as the water coming out the showerhead remained hot, which wasn't as long as he would have liked.

They dressed. Christine in her bikini and Tim in his Riptide shorts.

At the beach, they soaked in the morning sun and turned their skin a darker shade then it was the day before.

The waves crashed against rocks and sprayed a mist of salt water across them.

"It's so beautiful here," she said.

"You're beautiful."

"I think I can get used to this."

She rolled onto her side. He met her stare. She kissed him.

The morning crept along. They swam in the ocean and played as new lovers do.

Out in the blue warmth she floated on top of the water. He held her from underneath and the gentle rolling waves caused her body to move up and down in a rhythmic motion. She opened her eyes and he swam in her emerald greens. They were like a stiff drink and he was becoming intoxicated. Drunk with an emotion he couldn't fully comprehend.

He bent over and kissed her as the waves splashed water over them, around them, between them. The warm water was like a salty bath that defrosted his heart.

"You're amazing," he said as he pulled back.

"I'm fallen hard. Real hard."

After they patted off the water, he checked his watch.

Tim set up a Spa appointment for her for the rest of the day. He walked with her up the stairs that were encased in the rocks and kissed her good-bye.

The afternoon sun beat down a hot and humid 81 degrees. Sweat soaked the back of his head. He needed to take another dip and cool off.

He set up in the cave and placed the towels down on the loungers. The light bounced around the cave and flashed specks of white on the walls. He dove from the ledge and the water smothered him into its warmth. The sound above was muffled as the salt water engulfed him. He breeched the surface and into the hot Caribbean air.

The ladder attached to the volcanic rock held fast as he climbed its rungs. He pulled a towel from the chair and patted the water from his head.

The lounger was an invitation that he gladly accepted. The opening at the top of the cave let enough of the sun's rays to cook his skin. With his arms draped across the end of the lounger, he baked.

Behind the darkness of his eyelids, he found comfort. He couldn't remember a time in his life he had ever felt so relaxed. The urge to kill dulled inside him.

He opened his eyes and in front of him stood a pair of manicured toes. His eyes traced up her body. Toned, tanned legs shaped upward into the v-shaped area of the yellow bikini bottoms. A red ruby attached to the front of a small bellybutton sparkled. Her bare breasts were out in the open for the world to see. Small, but perky, red nipples stood erect as a warm breeze wafted in from the mouth of the cave. Orange lip-gloss coated her thin lips. The dial turned and the soft hum rose to a full vibration inside him.

"You like the view, Tim?" Rebecca asked.

"I've seen better."

"Oh really. I doubt that."

"So where's your husband?"

"Sleeping. Where's your girlfriend?"

"At the spa."

She sat down on the lounger beside him and placed her hand on the small of his back.

"Now, why would she leave a hot man like you all alone? I would never do that."

"Is that right? Then why are you not in bed with your man right now?"

"I said a hot man."

Her hand moved up and down his spine. Her fingernails trailed just above his skin and as she pulled away, she scratched him.

"You like that, Tim?"

Inside he was burning and it took every ounce of will to control the need. What he would like to do? Oh, what he would like to do to her.

He rose up from the lounger as swift as the breeze and pulled Rebecca into him. Her tits flattened bellow his chest. Their faces were close enough that their lashes touched. His hungry eyes pulled in her stare. He pushed her hard up against the rock wall. Tim was sure that he broke some skin. She growled back.

"You like it rough, huh? That's good. So do I."

"If I were you I would be very careful."

"Oh yeah. Or what? You going to hurt me, Tim?"

He pushed hard and her head snapped back against the wall with a thud.

"Hey! What the fuck!"

"I think you would be smart, if you took your tiny ass out of here."

"What's your problem? If you're not into it, just say so. You don't have to be an asshole."

"No, I think I will pass on the offer, but thanks," Tim said.

"What a shame..." she said and turned around.

He had a full view of her ass and the string buried between her cheeks. He needed a cold shower.

He entered the room as Christine was tying the end of the wrap around her waist.

"How was the spa?" he said.

"I feel like a new woman. The massage was fantastic. I forgot what it felt like to be knot free. I feel like Jell-O. Check out my nails."

He held her hand in his. The pink polish looked sexy on her. On the tips were small pictures of parrots. At first, he thought it looked cheesy but after a second and third glance, it grew on him.

"Looks great. Suits you."

"Thanks babe," she said.

"So what do you feel like doing today? Pool or Ocean?" she asked.

"Pool, I had too much salt water today and it left a bad taste in my mouth."

"Ok, whatever you think. I'm good either way."

"I'm going to take a shower I want to get the salt off. Care to join me?"

He caught her gaze and they were both in sync. Her hand slid across her flat stomach and undid the knot she had just tied. The wrap fell to the floor. He slipped out of his swim shorts, folded them, and placed them on the bed. Christine's bikini top fell to the pile building beneath her.

They never made it to the shower. Instead, they spent the afternoon tangled in the king-size bed.

Later that evening, dark grey clouds hovered out over the light blue ocean as they sat in the loungers at the bar. The first sign of rain came as a thin mist that covered Tim's shoulders and he could see the wetness absorb into Christine's hair. It felt refreshing.

The table was full of empty glasses. Today no matter how much he drank, he couldn't catch a buzz. Christine on the other hand was doing just fine. They were on the seventh round and she was coming out of her shell. Her white jacket spotted with light grey dots as the rain droplets hit the material. Her face was bright and the smile that spread across the wide reaching sides of her face cast a spell over him. It was hard to resist the invisible hand that tickled the back of his neck at every glance she shot toward him.

The wind picked up and lifted the cloth of the umbrella above. Her long hair moved in the breeze and flipped around her face. He wouldn't care if the clouds opened and rivers of rain splashed over them.

"You know Tim...," she said

"What?"

"I like you. I really like you. You know that?" she said.

Her hand reached for his and almost missed but he grabbed it before it slipped below the table. "You're a great guy. You know?"

"You're so different Christine. I mean, you bring something out of me that I've never felt before. It's like..."

"It's like your falling and you can't help yourself. You just want to keep falling. You love the feeling... right?" she said.

"Sure. Something, just like that."

He looked down at their hands entwined. Her one hand in his and the other in her lap. The hand on his shoulders was no apparition. It slid along his left shoulder, passing over the back of his neck, resting on his right side. Christine's eyes moved from his and lifted up. She was looking past him and over his head to whoever was standing behind him. The voice was calm as it spoke and he recognized the tone. It unmistakable. It was Rebecca's.

"Christine. I think you and I need to talk," Rebecca said.

THIRTY-FIVE

Jefferies understood two things: one, he needed his wife back. And two, he needed a break from the job. He was relieved that they had closed the case, but the empty apartment was like a coma. He felt like punching something.

He flipped the photo album's page and in the wedding pictures, he and his wife looked happy. He didn't recognize the man in the photo. That man smiled. That man was young and full of drive. The world was open to him and the future held the dreams that the newlyweds would soon plan.

Now, fifteen years later, the dreams shattered and the pieces floated around in his mind. *How did it get so far off track? How could he do that to his family? To Teresa? To Sarah?* All the signs were there if he would have just opened his eyes and looked. The missed dinners, the missed recitals, and the forgotten anniversaries. He could picture the many looks of disappointment on Teresa's face. The drained reflections. How many times she tried to talk to him. *Why the hell did he not go to counseling when she suggested it? He was a detective for fuck sakes.* The most important thing in the world was family and it was so easy for him to take it for granted.

He dialed the number. It rang once, twice and on the third ring, she answered.

"Hello?" she said.

For a moment, he wanted to hang up. His heart pounded in his chest and a lump formed in his throat, like quick-dry cement.

"Hi."

"Hi," she said.

Her voice was cold and hesitant. It killed him to hear it. It was like speaking with an old acquaintance. *What do you say? So much time has passed.* The distant feelings were hard to grasp.

"Baby, I'm so sorry. Please let me say what I have to say. Please hear me out."

"Go on," she said.

"I know what I've done to you and to my little girl. I hate myself for not seeing it sooner. I can't believe you didn't leave before. I should have opened up. I don't know why it happened but all I know is, that I tried to protect you from evil I see every day. By doing that, I created a wall between us. The more I packed everything away deep inside, the angrier I got. It must have been so hard for you. So difficult."

The tears streamed down his face and snot ran from his nose. "Baby...Baby I'm so fucking sorry...I'm so sorry."

He could hear her sniffing on the other end of the line. It was faint, but it was there and mixed in with his. They cried together and time slowed as the dam broke.

"I'm going to go to counseling. I'm going to get some help. I can't lose you and Sarah. I'll do whatever it takes. I'll quit the job if that's what I have to do. I'll do anything."

"I don't know," she said. "This is all so much. Damn it! Why did it take you so long? Why didn't you do this years ago? When I needed you to?"

"Baby, please? Please try? Come home. We'll do it together," he said.

The seconds slowed as he waited for her response. He could hear her breathing through the receiver. His stomach felt as if a knife was turning its sharp blade inside. A sudden rush of tears streamed from his eyes. *It's over. I've done too much damage. Oh, my God it's over. It's over. Oh my God, what have I done?*

"If you get some help. If you can bring back the man I fell in love with, then I will come home."

"Oh baby. I will. I'll call today. I would drive there right now if could."

"For all of us, I hope so. I'll give you a couple of months. My sister will let us stay here. You get your help and you call me when you're ready. We'll be here waiting when you do," she said.

"Ok, that's fair. Thank you. I miss you guys."

"We miss the old you. You go get him now." She said. Then hung up.

He placed the phone on the sofa cushion. He was exhausted but the weight lifted and he collapsed back in the warm leather glove of the sofa.

He cried.

In the kitchen, he looked through the department directory and found the extension of the department counselor. He hoped she would be able to fit him in as soon as possible. He had a couple of months to pull himself back together and the sooner he started the better.

In the hallway, his department issue Blackberry cried out. The sound was disturbing and he tried to pretend he hadn't heard it. But, it rang out again. *Fucking leave me alone. Leave me alone.*

THRTY-SIX

Rebecca smirked at Christine. Her rain soaked hair clung to her face like sea kelp.

"Talk about what?" Christine said.

The water dripped from Christine's hair and onto her white jacket, which was quickly turning grey. Tim could tell by the look in her eyes that she was livid.

"Well, did he tell about our little encounter today?" Rebecca asked.

Christine's eyes flashed from above Tim's head and locked onto his own. The expression chilled him and he didn't like the look.

"I think you better leave." Tim said.

Rebecca's fingernails dug into his shoulder pinching through his soaked shirt.

"You gonna hit me again, Tim? Go ahead. You know I like it."

He pushed his chair back slamming the back of it into Rebecca's legs.

"Hey! Watch it, Asshole," she said as she slid away from him and moved toward Christine.

"What the fuck is going on here?" Christine said.

Tim grabbed Rebecca hard and pushed her away from Christine. He moved fast, ushering Rebecca out of the bar and toward the pathway. She shouted out in disgust. He looked back, and Christine was slow to get up from the affects of the alcohol.

He moved his mouth close enough to Rebecca's ear and from behind, it would look as if he was kissing it.

"Listen, because I'll only say this once. Leave the resort tonight, or, come morning, you will be dead." He tightened his grip on her arms. It must have hurt like hell because Tim held her entire weight as her knees buckled.

With Rebecca well on her way down the pathway, he turned back toward the bar. Christine was waiting with her hand on the table. She used the chair to support herself. The rain slowed to a mere drizzle as the moon pushed through a break in the clouds. Her skin looked a touch green but her eyes flashed crimson.

"What was that?" she yelled.

"She's a lunatic. A fucking slut. That's all. Just forget about it."

He slipped a hand around the back of her neck. Her skin was cold and wet. She pushed his hand away.

"I want to know right now. Right now!"

For the first time in a long time, he was at a loss for words. He just stood there with his mouth half open.

"Well! I'm waiting," she said.

"Christine, let's go to bed. You're drunk and I'm not in the mood to argue."

"I'm not going anywhere until you tell me."

She tried to move the chair around to sit on it and he caught her before she fell over.

"Fine, while I was swimming in the cave this afternoon she tried to seduce me. I made it clear that I wanted nothing to do with her. That's it and that's all there is to say about."

"Why didn't you tell me?" Christine said. She folded her arms across her chest as she shot him a look that would have made any other man wince.

"I handled things my own way and I didn't see any reason to tell you. Rebecca is a leach and her type is only happy when other people are miserable," he said.

"That changes nothing. Handle shit your way if that's what you do. But Tim, I don't like being blindsided. It's the one thing that pisses me off."

THIRTY-SEVEN

Tim was unravelling. Waves of confusion left him wandering through the depths of his mind like an explorer on a newfound continent. The concrete pathways dried from the hot air as the remnants of the storm floated off of the path like a ghost in the breeze. He slapped a wood post and the light that hung from the post swayed splashing shadows across the path.

Inside he boiled over with intensity that was hard for him to control. The argument loosened the code he lived by. The string that held him together. Rebecca, he could manage but Christine was different. He felt something for her. And that something battled within. Ann was the last woman that could affect him emotionally and he had handled her. Now, it was back again. Emotions that he had buried so deep that he thought the devil himself could not excavate them.

His hand throbbed as a reminder that he needed to control his anger. There would be consequences for acting on emotion. Remember...control, analytics, and pace. Relax.

Breathe.

The villa was up to the right on the tip of the cliff. In the distance, the lighthouse glowed in the night as a beacon of hope. He reached the door of their room. He tried the doorknob. It was locked.

Around the back, the waves crashed into the rocks below. Tim moved along the back patio. The moon reflected off the explosion of white water and the impression was unnerving. It looked like an army of white sprits charging forward. He shook the thought from his mind and moved toward the back window. It was open. The curtain blew in and out: a waving of the white flag. *Not tonight.*

The room was a mirror image of the villa that he rented: the same four-poster bed and the same mural above.

A man snored loud enough to stop Tim in his tracks. It boomed, snorted, and sounded like a cow on its last breath. Rebecca lay beside her husband. She was naked from the waist up. Her clean white panties glowed in the dark room. Her neck looked exceptionally small. Fragile.

How easy it would be to slip his hand around it and squeeze. It wouldn't take much, just a flex of his bicep, and a few seconds later *pop*. Maybe she would open her eyes and maybe she wouldn't. It didn't matter. She would be dead and that would be good.

Excellent.

He backed away from the bed and sat in the chair in the corner of the room. He was masked by the darkness as he pondered his next move. His rage guided him to her room, his inner voice directing. Here he was with fire burning in his veins. Rebecca had done something to him. She had placed a wedge, between him and Christine. It was uncalculated on his part and it had come from out of nowhere.

The distance between Rebecca and him was only a few feet. He could cross the void and it would be done in seconds. He could kill her without waking the husband. His urges would be cleansed and he would feel renewed. Then there was Christine. She was a cop. She would figure it out. The detective in her would see through him. See him for who he was. What he does. Now his actions were governed by the morals and rules of another.

Tim needed sleep. He wore the day's events like a wetsuit. He couldn't shed it. It was caked with ocean salt and the zipper was stuck.

He slipped out the window, leaving the woman alive and his mind at odds, but the decision was made.

In life, two things were certain: life and death. The latter he controlled. Death was easy. It was certain. It was something he controlled but living was a whole other matter. Regardless of his decision at this point, Christine was a part of his life. That was something he wanted, no matter the outcome.

He laid down beside Christine and their skin touched. The hot sweat soaked his skin. She smelled like a fresh flower: a lilac or a rose, her life in his hands and his in hers. Together they would find the path that would guide them to something more than he could imagine.

The years he spent with Ann, at this point, seemed like a dream, one last nightmare. And with Christine, he could be something. Anything. Her breathing was rhythmic. It moved as the wind moved through the window. The warm Jamaican breeze flowed in through the window like a thief in the night. There, then gone.

The next day was not as he expected, Christine woke with only a fog of the events that played out the day prior. She could remember only bits and pieces.

"What happened last night? Was I dreaming or did a woman really cause a fight between us?"

He had checked with the operator and Rebecca and her husband had left first thing that morning. She had taken the warning seriously. That was good. Because if she spent one more night here, he wasn't sure, he could control the outcome. He asked the manager for a favor and after adding a hundred dollars to the request the manager agreed and gave him the information he needed. He may visit her one day for a little retribution.

"It was nothing. She was drunk and she was flirting with me. I handled it," he said. He wrapped his arm around her breasts and folded it underneath her, pulling her into his chest. He loved the way she looked naked. Like something he would put on canvas, if he could paint.

"Oh. Sorry I got drunk last night," She said.

"Don't worry about it."

It looked like the storm was over. He thanked the alcohol for that. Faded memories. He wanted more from Christine.

THIRTY-EIGHT

"Christine. It's Jeffries. I hope you're enjoying your time off. Look, we're back on the Picasso case. Crazy I know...but the FBI needs to pull back some of their resources and asked if we would assist them. Just give me a call when you get the message." He placed the receiver back in the base, rubbed his hand through his hair, and leaned back into the chair. Just when he thought he would be able to focus on Teresa and work on his issues the job interfered once again.

He didn't buy it for one minute. His gut was telling him that Lawson was good for this. He knew it. Like an addict with a drug-fever, he was certain that Lawson made a mistake. It was inevitable—like a mouse stealing cheese—there was bound to be a trail and Jeffries was convinced he would find it.

He flipped open the folder containing Lawson's alibis and started from the top.

Later, the frustration surged inside him after the third call ended in more disappointment. He dialed the number of the hotel in Paris. Lawson stayed there during the murder at St. Patrick's Cathedral. He waited the few seconds it took for someone to pick up on the other end. He looked at his watch it read 12:38pm; it would be 6:38pm in Paris. After the fourth ring, a French voice answered.

"This is Detective Jeffries of the New York Police Department I'm calling from Manhattan. May I speak to the hotel manager, please?"

"Yes, one second sir," a woman's voice said with a strong French accent.

He scribbled on the note pad as he waited.

"Hello, this is Monsieur Vasser. How can I help you?"

"Mr. Vasser, I'm Detective Jeffries. I'm calling from Manhattan. I'm investigating a murder and I was hoping you could help me with something."

"Certainly," he said.

"I have notes that your hotel confirmed to the FBI that one Mr. Lawson, was a guest at your hotel on October 14th 2007. Could you verify this for me?"

"One second, Sir."

Jeffries could hear typing on the other end of the line. The manager must be checking the dates. A thought occurred to him as he drew a line connecting the stars he drew to the happy face he scribbled on the notepad.

"Mr. Vasser, Mr. Vasser."

"One second. Ok detective. Yes, we do have a Mr. Lawson checking in on the 14th and checking out on the 16th."

"Is it possible to speak with the hotel clerk that checked Mr. Lawson into the hotel?"

"Yes, Mr. Lawson stayed at our hotel,"

"Mr. Vasser, thank you but I believe I asked you if I could speak with the hotel clerk that checked in Mr. Lawson."

"I'm sorry, you said what?"

"Oh for Christ sakes, can I speak with the clerk that checked Mr. Lawson into the hotel?"

"Sir, there is no need for hostility. One second, he is with a customer. Please hold."

Jeffries broke the tip of the pencil, threw the pencil aside, and pulled a pen from the metal wire cup next to his monitor.

"Hello?"

"Who am I a speaking to?" Jeffries said.

"This is Marcel."

"Marcel, did your manager explain why I need to speak with you?"

"Yes."

"Good. Now on October 14th you checked in Mr. Lawson correct?"

"Yes and no," said the clerk.

"What do you mean yes and no? What are you talking about?"

"Mr. Lawson's credit card was used to reserve and pay for the room but I did not check in a Mr. Lawson."

"Huh?"

"Mr. Lawson did not show up. Instead, a woman checked in under his reservation. I remember this because I had to call Mr. Lawson for confirmation."

"So Mr. Lawson never showed?"

"That is correct, sir."

"And you know this how?"

"Because, sir, I checked the woman out myself and she used her credit card to cover the hotel incidentals."

Jefferies' mind coiled like a serpent ready to strike. *Got em!*

"Tell your manager that I'll be talking with the Paris police. They will be sending over a warrant for that information. In the mean time, please write down what you told me. We're going to need a copy of your signed statement and a copy of that hotel bill as well."

"Yes sir, I will do so."

"Thank you Marcel. You just made my day."

"You're welcome sir."

***

Lawson clicked on the hidden folder marked "exhibits" and scanned through the articles of his masterpiece collection. He felt like he was unstoppable. Brilliant.

Each article was filed in order.

He noticed the soft ring tone coming from the office phone. He checked the caller I.D. and it was the Paris hotel phoning.

"Lawson," he said as he answered the call.

"Mr. Lawson this is Monsieur Vasser calling from Hotel Scribe, Paris."

"Yes?"

"Well forgive me for calling sir but I have to tell you that a detective called me just now inquiring about one of your recent reservations. Personally, I detest how you American's invade people's privacy. I'm not referring to you of course but of your terrible institution, you call government. Anyway, this is just a courtesy call as you are one of our guests and I thought you should know."

"Mr. Vasser I appreciate the call. Would you mind giving me the name of the detective that called you?"

"Certainly. His name is Detective Jeffries of the New York Police Department."

"Thank you Mr. Vasser," Lawson said.

Lawson placed the handset back into the base. His mind raced as he tried to establish a plan for damage control. Only minutes before he was in the free and clear. Now, they had broken one of his alibis and soon he was sure they would crack the rest.

After ten minutes of planning, he hit a roadblock. His breathing quickened and his entire body tensed. He curled his hands into tight fists, raised them above his head, and then slammed them onto the hard oak desk with enough force to cause a hairline crack in the wood.

Within seconds, his door opened and his assistant poked her head in. She looked concerned.

"Get out," he said.

She closed the door before the words ceased to vibrate in his ears.

He was stuck. He envisioned his world crashing around him. He would lose everything he'd worked so hard to build. His anger filled every ounce of him.

Jeffries and Christine would pay. They now owed him their lives and he was going to collect.

Over the next two hours, he wrote down his plan on a sheet of foolscap with a number two pencil. He created a list of items that he would need to be executed with laser accuracy and perfect timing. One slip and he would be behind bars and locked away from everything he lived for.

THIRTY-NINE

The drive to the airport was cold and quiet. Reflections of the last few days played out in Tim's mind like an old black and white movie. The characters rolled through their parts without a single word or phrase but the actions rang out like the town hall bell casting shadows of negative feelings.

The last two days were extremely frustrating and not what he had planned. He wanted them to be like the first few, full of affection and intimacy. Instead, they exchanged maybe thirty words at the most. After she woke up and had a coffee, her memory of the argument came back.

Christine could not let go of the Rebecca situation and she was as serious as a gunshot wound when it came to being slighted. She had made that clear. He handled her as best he could but she remembered him becoming violent with Rebecca and this scared her she told him.

She questioned him about Rebecca's comment about *him hitting her again,* and he lied to her about that and said that Rebecca was making it up. Inside he knew she didn't buy it. Tim hoped she would have forgotten what happened. He was sadly mistaken. She remembered everything.

The view through the window of the Lincoln was surreal; the huts along the side of the road were dilapidated. Steel roofs looked like they were dropped on top of concrete blocks. The cement between the cinders eroded and large gaps gave the look that the huts would fall in with the slightest breeze. Amazing that they stood up to hurricanes. Funny that expensive trucks and cars were parked in front of the make shift homes.

"If they own nice cars, then what's with the houses?" Christine asked.

The comment was directed toward the driver, and not to Tim.

"Da government own da land. An day can kick ya off when dem see fit," the driver said. "Hard da live like dat. So da kar is da only ting ya keeps," he added.

They arrived at the airport in forty minutes and the cold atmosphere in the vehicle made it feel more like two lifetimes. Tim tipped the driver and paid a red cap to transport their luggage to the private jet, which waited for them on the tarmac.

"Christine don't you think you're taking this a little too far?" Tim said, as they trailed the Red Cap and their luggage.

"Hey, you were the one that lied." Christine said.

"I didn't lie to you. I chose to deal with it myself."

"And why won't you tell me what you said to her as you were dragging her out of the bar? Huh, what about that?" she said.

Her tone rose as a jet taxied for takeoff. He was finished arguing. The woman was just in a state of anger that he couldn't charm her out of. He would wait it out. She would come around. They always did. It wasn't like he slept with Rebecca. In fact, he did the right thing. Christine was displaying the New York attitude and he was used to it.

He dropped Christine off as the sun washed the skyscrapers red and set Manhattan a glow. She gave him a quick hug and thanked him for the trip.

FORTY

Christine woke the next day stressed and felt like she lost something. Her muscles were knotted back up again and she could hardly remember the massage she had received only a few days ago. By the time Tim dropped her off last night, she was exhausted from the travel, and all she could think about was what Rebecca said about him. The memory of how he handled the woman scared her. Not because she herself, was afraid of him. It was that he could be like that. He could be angry to the point where he became physical and she'd seen too many spousal abuse cases to ignore it. It was just sad. So sad.

She cried.

Opening her suitcase, she was reminded of Tim's generosity. The items he bought for her filled her new case. She unpacked all her new clothes and she put them aside in a pile. She would give the clothes back to him. It was the right thing to do. She looked at the outfits and was saddened. They were all so beautiful and it killed her that she had to break it off. *But what else could she do?*

She called the union representative and he confirmed her appointment with the psychologist for her "Fit-for-Duty" evaluation. She could return to active duty after he gives her the green light. He asked if she had a fun time on her trip and Christine shrugged off the question and never answered him.

They hung up, and she called Tim.

He wasn't home so she tried his cell. He answered on the first ring.

"Hey, I was just thinking about you," he said.

"Hi, Tim. Can you meet me today?"

"Sure, do you want me to come over?"

"No. Let's get a coffee. Can you meet at the Starbucks near my place?"

"Sure. What's up? Is something wrong? You sound different."

"I'm Ok. Can you be there in an hour?"

"I'll see you then," he said.

She hung up.

Christine had taken lots of photos with her digital camera and she loaded them into her laptop. They flashed up, one by one as the hourglass rotated on the screen. Tears filled her eyes and ran down her cheeks as she looked at the photos.

With breakfast, which consisted of yogurt and toast, she was off.

Outside, her long hair flapped in the cold wind as she walked toward the Starbucks holding the bag. This winter's colors were red or black and she fit right in with her long black coat. The faces that passed her on the street had either that look that someone just took a shit or it's my birthday and fuck you if you don't like it attitude.

She opened the door and she saw Tim sitting at the chairs in the back, with two coffee cups on the table. She moved through the line-up.

He got up as she approached and he hugged her. She held him and she didn't want to let go. She could smell his cologne and a tear crept into the corner of her eye. She took the empty chair beside him and placed the bag between her feet.

"Hey," he said.

"Hi."

"What's in the bag?" he said.

She avoided the question, "We have to talk."

"This doesn't sound good."

"Tim, I think you're a great guy."

"I think you're great too."

"The problem is…well, I don't know how to say this without hurting your feelings but I have to say it anyway and believe me it's killing me to do this."

"Christine, what's wrong?"

"I don't think we should see each other anymore," and as she said the words two tears rolled down her cheeks.

"What? Why?"

"I just can't do it. I don't think you would ever hurt me but I can't be with a man that has anger issues."

"What are talking about? You think I have issues? Christine, I would never hurt you."

"I know that, inside, but the cop in me Tim is guiding my decision. I've seen too many times how angry people can be. I've seen the results of that anger and I just can't be around that. I'm sorry."

She watched as something changed in his expression. He was calm. It felt odd.

"Is that the clothes I bought you?"

"Yes."

What happened next surprised the hell out of her. He rose out of the chair, picked up the bag, and left without another word.

Minutes later, she left the Starbucks shaken.

In the department psychologist's office, she sat across from him in a soft brown leather chair.

He ran through a list of questions. She answered honestly. She handed him a copy of the police report and he followed along listening intently as she explained the events that occurred the day she shot Simone Adams.

Afterward, he asked her to answer a Fit-for-Duty questionnaire, which she did and all the while, he watched her. She thought about the perception fellow officers share about this process and it's no wonder they don't trust the system. It's maddening know if they reveal too much about what they are truly thinking, they could be pulled from their unit.

The entire interview lasted two hours and he informed her that she would hear back from the union rep regarding the results.

FORTY-ONE

Struggle. A slippery word that described how he was feeling. The loss of control and handing the reins that directed his emotions over to another. A thing that only one other woman had ever held. Ann. She was the only one, up until now, that could ever control him. That could break his heart and sadden his mind. He had broken free and by following his own rules, had never let that happen again.

But, now, the truth was as sure as the cold blade rolling across his palm, the truth was, Christine held the reigns. What scared him the most was not that she held that much power over his emotions. No, not from the loss of control. It was that he liked it. He liked her. Maybe loved her. If he even knew what that meant, and now she had ended it.

He finished typing the email and sent the email off, traveling among the millions sent across the World Wide Web. Within seconds, it would reach Christine's inbox.

He was careful not to say too much but just enough. He rose from his desk walked over to the bookshelf. He scanned through his CD collection and found the Reservoir Dogs' sound track. He played Steelers Wheel's "Stuck in the Middle With You". The familiar song he remembered from his childhood. The movie was another one of his favorites and the song always brought back the image of Michael Madsen cutting a cops ear off.

His inbox flashed and the bold number one appeared at the end of the Inbox button. It read:

To:tim@clu.net
From:cmaloan@nypd.31.gv.com
Subject: re: Us
Hi Tim, I'm sorry too!

I read your email and I wish I had another answer for you. I agree we just met and I agree that I think we have learned so much about each other over the last month. I really liked you Tim. It's hard for me to meet someone that can understand the "job", you know what I mean. You did. I was so happy about that. I think that you and I did have a lot in common and there was so much more we could have learned.

Tim, after I got back I thought about what happened with Rebecca and I understand now that you did what you had to because that's how you handle stuff like that. I wish you had told me before about your mother, and how she treated you. Then, at least, I would have been more understanding. Every day I see violence and I know that all of us have it in us to become violent. But Tim you're a man now and those events were a long time ago. But that doesn't change the fact that you have an anger problem.

You don't have to apologize to me regarding Rebecca. In my eyes, now that I know what I know about it, I do understand. But, I'm sorry, that doesn't change how I feel and I don't think we can be together.

I don't regret meeting you and I will always remember you.

Christine

Tim closed the lid of his Mac and threw it across the room. It smashed into the wall and fell to the floor. The weight of a thousand elephants hung from his shoulders.

He moved back from the chair and climbed the spiral staircase to his upstairs loft.

In his bedroom, he pulled out a black leather bag from his closet.

***

Later that night, he knocked on Samantha's door. She answered wearing a black dress. She looked like she had been crying.

"Tim, what are you doing here?"

"Can I come in?"

She rubbed her hand through her hair, "I'm sorry. Where are my manners? Please come on in."

He moved through the door and she closed it behind him. He followed her into the kitchen and she picked up an empty glass stained with red wine.

"Would you like a glass?" she asked.

"I would love one. Thank you."

She pulled the cork from the bottle, poured a glass, and handed it to him. Then filled her empty one.

"I didn't see you at the funeral." She said.

"I know. I'm sorry. I just don't do well at funerals."

He thought of Simone in her casket and wondered what her family must have thought when they found out that she was a killer. He sipped the wine.

"I see. Did the police contact you?"

"No. Why?"

"Oh. No reason. I just thought that since you were close to her they may have had some questions for you."

"No, they didn't contact me. Did you give them my name? It's ok if you did."

"No. Besides the name *Tim*, that's all we knew about you."

He was happy to hear her answer. He wasn't sure how he would explain to Christine about his relationship with Simone. He was sure his lie would hold up but he didn't want to have that conversation.

"So, why are you here?" she asked.

"I want to talk to you about Simone. To try and understand."

"Honestly Tim, we were just surprised as I'm sure you were. It's all fucked up. My parents are crushed."

"So, where's Doug?"

"He's working late. He should be home soon."

"Oh," he said.

"I don't know what to tell you. Other than I guess I'm sorry for you as well."

He watched as she reached across the table and squeezed his hand. He held it as they both drank from their glasses, and returned them to the table empty.

The phone rang and Samantha got up from the table to answer it.

He refilled their drinks.

After a quick conversation, she ended the call and returned to the table.

"That was Doug. He's going to be couple of hours. You're welcome to stay if you want too. I just don't feel like being alone right now."

Tim nodded.

"Simone told me that you ran an art gallery." He said

"It's weird talking about her. I knew about your visit to the MET. She thought you were some big art expert."

"I'm not."

"She said you showed her some ghost in a Picasso painting. Is that actually true?"

He nodded.

"It's amazing that I've never heard about it. Which painting was it?"

"*The Old Guitarist.* The first time I saw it, I was on a field trip. We were visiting an art gallery and it caught my eye because I also play guitar. When I looked close. I mean real close. I noticed a light shadow in the background. At first, I thought it was an illusion. But she was there. It was an image of a lady hidden in the background underneath the layers of oil."

"That's interesting... Did you mean what you said?" she asked.

"When?"

"When you were here a while back."

"About what?"

"About me. About how I looked."

He wasn't sure how it happened; maybe it was the wine or maybe it was just how Samantha grieved but soon after the second bottle, her expression changed and she hugged him for a long time. The heat from her face warmed his cheek and he kissed her. She kissed him back. They both pulled away and stared at one another. Then kissed again.

He pulled her up into his arms and sat her on the kitchen table. The wine bottle fell over and a splash of wine stained the white oak. He felt her hand on his cock as she stroked overtop of his jeans. He kissed her hard on the mouth as he hiked her dress up above her thighs. She was breathing warm breaths into his ear as she kissed it. He slipped her panties down her legs and let them drop to the floor below. He was inside her and she was moaning. She wrapped her legs around his waist and rocked into him.

After, they both sat at the kitchen table. Neither said a word. He just stared at her in amazement of what had just happened. He saw her look down at her panties on the floor. She bent over, picked them up, and held them in her closed fist.

"Doug will be home soon. You should probably go."

"Does he know I'm here?"

"Yes, but he won't care if you don't stay. I'll tell him you had to leave."

"Ok."

"Let's keep this between us," she said.

He wasn't sure why she said that. Who would he tell? The comment was weird but he took that as a cue to leave. Funny, he came here to kill her and in the end, he was glad he didn't. It would have complicated things.

"Thanks for the wine," he said as he walked to the door.

"Thanks for the conversation," she said as she closed it.

FORTY-TWO

"Good to have you back," Jeffries said.

"Good to be back," Christine said.

They both sat down at her desk and he must have noticed something.

"You look like you've been crying," he said.

"Oh."

"Yep. You want to talk about it."

"I broke it off with Tim."

"Sorry to hear. You ok?"

"I'll be alright. So what happened with you and Teresa?"

"I promised her that I'll go to counseling and that I would open up."

"That's great. I'm really happy for you. So what's next?" She asked.

The Captain interrupted their conversation. He handed Jeffries a note. He read it without responding.

Finished reading, he placed the note on his desk, and then slapped Christine on the leg.

"We got him! We fucking got him!"

"Who'd we get?" she said.

"Didn't you get my message?"

"No. What message?"

"The one I left on your voicemail."

"Haven't checked it."

"It's a long story but we're back on the Picasso Case."

"When did that happen?"

"Last week. I broke his alibis. We have a warrant out for his arrest and the note the Captain just handed me contained his whereabouts. Lawson's SUV was spotted at a motel in Brooklyn.

Whoop. The launcher ejected a projectile that sailed through the air. The glass shattered. Behind the broken window, the room filled with smoke. The rusted numerals on the door read 22. The numbers bounced as the battering ram crashed through the door and the door swung back against the far wall.

Two members of SWAT breached the entrance as Christine caught the flicker of light out of the corner of her eye. She turned in time to see the black SUV peel out of the parking lot.

"Jeffries, get in," she said.

He hesitated and she slapped on the roof of the car. The noise sent him in motion and he jumped into the Charger. Before both doors could shut, she pushed the accelerator to the floor. The back end shifted. The nose of the Charger turned out onto Emmons Avenue and out of the Comfort Inn parking lot.

Ahead, she could see the taillights of the SUV turning right onto Shore Parkway. She followed up the ramp and swerved into the empty lane. The large vehicle weaved in and out of the line of cars ahead. They were now about four vehicle lengths behind and closing.

"What are you going to do? You going to ram him?" Jeffries said.

"No way. What if he rolls? Can't take that chance. Someone might get hurt."

She pulled in behind a Toyota and two-car lengths back from the SUV. She heard Jeffries calling for back up and he requested a helicopter as well.

"We're going to follow him. We'll pick him up when he stops. Cool?" She said.

"Cool," Jefferies said.

They followed the SUV off the Belt Parkway onto a side street. The unnamed road led them past four parked cars and ended in a roundabout. The SUV sat idling in the front entrance to a rest stop. The driver's side door was wide open and the vehicle looked empty or seemed that way from her vantage point.

She stopped the car and they both slid out closing the car doors behind them. She approached the SUV with her gun drawn. Jeffries gave her the thumbs up from behind the SUV. Christine crouched down and peered into the driver's side door.

"Empty," she said.

The SUV's engine grunted to a stop as Christine removed her hand from the vehicle holding the keys. She shut the door and locked the vehicle.

"You head around back and I'll take the front," she pointed to the front doors of the rest stop.

He moved out of sight and back down the far left wall. Christine took three steps and placed her back against the cold concrete. The steel doors were painted grey and she could see the damage of time underneath a fresh coat of paint. She pulled at the handle and the door screeched in protest, as it swung open. Inside, a door with the word restrooms was on the far wall. To her right, the visitor's main office door looked locked and the light was out.

She moved to the wall to her left and slid up to the door. She pushed through, crouching and ready to fire. The hallway was empty and the only sound she heard was the beating of her own heart.

At the far end of the hall underneath the exit sign, the door opened and sunlight poured in. She exhaled as Jeffries moved in from the light and she took the pressure off of the trigger. He was moving his head from side to side as if to say *he didn't see anything.* She waved to him and he moved in her direction.

The sound of running water came from inside the Men's washroom. This made Christine jump and she pulled Jefferies beside her. Together they pushed through.

"Don't fucking move," Jefferies said.

She was surprised to see Lawson standing at the sink. Just standing there. He was the width of two mirrors and then some. His black jacket rippled around his oversized arms. *Why is he fucking smiling?*

"I was wondering when you were going to gather enough nerve to come in here," Lawson said.

"Been running for while, huh, Lawson? Well that will be the end of that. Christine, you shoot him if he makes a move," Jefferies said.

She covered Jeffries as he moved toward Lawson. Lawson turned around and placed his hands behind his head as if in a good faith gesture. Christine moved the sight of her gun above Jefferies and on to the back of Lawson's head.

"It's ok, Detective. I don't bite," Lawson said.

Jeffries took his cuffs out and reached up to take Lawson's wrist.

Christine fired off a shot that sailed by Lawson's right ear but it was too late and millimeters off the mark. Lawson had Jeffries in a chokehold; His feet dangled about six inches off of the ground. His face was turning red and his eyes looked like they were going to burst from their sockets. She fired another round this time grazing Lawson's left temple.

"Christine, take another shot and I'll break his fucking neck. Drop your gun!"

"I'm not dropping my gun. Put him down or I swear I'll put two in your balls before I put one between your eyes," she said.

"Well, I think we're at a stalemate. Personally, I have nothing to lose. Either, I go to jail or you kill me. You unfortunately have a lot to lose. I'm not kidding, Detective. Put the gun down and kick it over here. Quickly... I can feel him going."

Christine watched Jeffery's face turn from red to a shade of blue from the lack of oxygen. With no other choice, she dropped the gun and kicked it toward Lawson. As the gun slid along the concrete, Lawson dropped her partner and Jeffries fell to the ground in a heap. From what she could tell, he wasn't breathing. Lawson moved toward her and that was the last thing she remembered until waking up in the cage.

FORTY-THREE

Tim paced the area between the kitchen and the living room. His mind raced as he tried to come up with a solution. He heard about Christine's kidnapping on the news and he was trying to devise a plan to get her back.

He opened the folder and scanned each document thoroughly to find something that would link Picasso to her. After twenty minutes, he came up empty. He ran his hands through his hair and looked up at the lofted ceiling. He had tried to forget Christine. She had left him and for days after he felt empty. He occupied his thoughts with Samantha and even started trolling again but something was missing and it was the first time he had felt anything like that. He played back every event in his mind and when he reached the night of their first date he realized that after all this time he had the answer. He had come face to face with 'The Picasso Killer' and his license plate number was stored in his Blackberry.

He slipped the phone from its holster at his side and found the file. He wrote the number down on a piece of paper and pinged Sandy.

The messenger program popped up on the Blackberry.

Sandy: Yo!

Tim: Hi Sandy. Did you get the file?

Sandy: And here I am? Who's James Lawson?

Tim: Damn you're quick. I need a list of all his properties.

Sandy: What for? He's not your type.

Tim: That's funny. That's why I like you.

Sandy: How come you never visit me anymore?

Tim: Not now. I need that information. ASAP.

Sandy: Fine. One sec.

Sandy: Ok. He has a house in the Hamptons, a condominium in Miami, I found warehouse in Manhattan, and a Cottage in Canada. Which one do you want?

He thought of the warehouse and that was a possible location but his instincts told him the cottage and he always trusted his gut.

Tim: Give me the cottage.

Sandy: Emailed you the map—should be in your inbox.

Tim: Need to get a gun across the Canadian border. Ideas?

Sandy: One sec.

Sandy: Ok you need an Authorization to Transport permit.

Tim: Great. How do I get one?

Sandy: Give me twenty minutes. Might take some heavy hacking. Nothing I can't handle. Check your email in bit!

Tim: Thank you Sandy. I'll see you when I see you.

He closed the messenger application and sure enough, the email box had one new message. It contained a map and direction from the closest airport. He thought of Sandy and smiled. She was good.

He called his travel agent and she arranged the chartered flight to Buttonville Airport, Toronto, Canada.

Upstairs, he placed the loaded Glock into his black leather bag, along with the eight-inch Bowie. The scarves he left in the closet. He zipped up the bag, closed the door, and climbed back down the spiral staircase. He checked his email again, found what he needed, and then printed off a copy.

He imagined what he would do to Christine if he were Lawson and the images made him shudder. He felt his skin heat up with tension and once again, he felt the urge.

He shook the thought from his mind, left his condominium, and moved toward the elevator. He wasn't sure what Lawson would do but, based on what he did to the other victims, it would be excruciatingly painful, and that enraged him.

At the airport, he tipped the taxi driver and followed the signs that directed him to a private hanger where he would catch his chartered flight.

FORTY-FOUR

Her knees hurt and her legs were stiff from the cramped space. She had an itch on the small of her back but was unable to scratch at it. Her wrists were handcuffed in front of her and the chain of the cuffs looped around the iron bars. The iron bars of the cage that held her.

The room was quiet. Just the sound of her own heartbeat played on the stage between her ears. Christine reached back to the memory of the bathroom. The image of Lawson holding Jeffries and the way her partner's body fell and crumbled to the floor. Lawson running at her and feeling like she was hit by a subway train. Then the black. The dark. Nothing, until now.

The noise and the vibration rattled her. She looked to the side. *Lawson!* His massive structure blacked out the room and his white dress shirt gripped his forearm like melted plastic as he ran a pipe over the bars.

"Well. Well. Isn't this a nice surprise," Lawson said.

"Fuck you, Lawson."

"I would say that's no way for a lady to talk, but there isn't one in the room."

Christine wanted to reach through the cage, grab him by his balls, and pull hard. Rip them from his body.

"Let's skip the niceties, shall we?" Lawson said.

"Please, I can't take any more. Hearing your voice is like eating shit," she said.

Lawson hit the bars again with the pipe. She recoiled from the sharp pain that shot through her teeth and up into her sinuses. "Shut your filthy mouth!"

He moved back from the cage and sat in the large recliner in front of her. She scanned the room. They were in an open dining room and to the left, a kitchen. The front door mocked her as if it was calling out to her and telling *her here I am, just open me, and you're free.*

She said nothing.

"Would you like it if I let you out of the cage?"

"Yes."

He reached over and stuck a key into the lock. She heard it click. His thick finger flipped the lock sideways and then he slipped the metal u-shape through the holes between the door and the cage. He hadn't moved from his seat to do it.

"There."

"What about the cuffs?" she asked.

"Oh. Those."

He slipped his hand into his shirt pocket and pulled out a key. He showed it to her. He brought it up real close. "If you want me to take those off, then you're going to have to do something for me."

"I figured you were like that. Explains why you remove the genitals. Sexual issues?"

He laughed. It startled her. She flinched and hit her head on the top of the cage. She tried to move her hand to touch her head and the steel cuff bit into her skin.

"Is that what you think?"

"You tell me."

"My appetite has nothing to do with sex. Trust me."

"What then?"

"I want to borrow your ear."

"You want to talk. Correct?"

"Of course. What else?" he asked.

"Ok. I'm listening."

"You seem like an intelligent woman. Competent."

He placed the steel pipe on the floor. It rolled across the wood and the noise sounded mechanical and unexpected. The pipe must have weighed five pounds. Maybe more. It stopped when it hit the edge of the oriental style rug.

"Like I said, I think you have a good head on your shoulders. I can appreciate that. It's comforting that you were the one that got close and not the FBI...You know Michael was a complete moron."

"I wouldn't expect someone like you to speak ill of the dead. And by the way, it wasn't me that broke your alibi."

"Whatever, it's inconsequential. A moot point really. I know it was Jefferies. Do you want to know why I picked you instead of him?"

"Do I have a choice?"

"Not really."

"Ok, Why?"

"A few reasons. I think you're in better shape than Jefferies for one and I can tell you have street smarts. You're quick, which makes for a more formidable opponent. A challenge."

"I thought you were going to take off the cuffs," she said.

"In due time. The first victim, the women on the water tower, do you want to know why I picked her?"

"Enlighten me!"

"Change your tone or I'll cut your tongue out."

She realized she was in trouble but for a second, just a second, she forgot that she was on the other end of the interrogation. She was the one handcuffed and locked in a cage. A cage that would be inhumane for dogs let alone a human being. "I'm sorry. Continue."

"That's better. She applied for a job. It was a marketing role within my company. She was a smart women. Like you, but attractive. No offence of course."

"None taken."

"I interviewed her. It went well. She was extremely qualified for the position. She put her best foot forward and I was considering her for the short list. Until she made the comment."

"Which comment was that?"

"She said, and these were her exact words, *"If you offer me the position. I can promise you that I will get results. But what I won't do is come to work without a bra. I'm sorry Mr. Lawson but if I'm going to work here, I will not be dressing like your assistant"* can you believe the nerve of her?"

"So that's why you killed her? That's why you cut off her breasts?"

"Wouldn't you?"

She felt vomit trickle up the back of her throat and swallowed it back.

"You see, you and I come from a different litter don't we? No need to answer. It's rhetorical.

"You're a murderer."

"Of course. And so are you. I read about your little ordeal with Simone Adams. Killing a defenseless woman."

"Defenseless...she fired four rounds at us!"

"Still. She had no training unlike you or your partner. You could have waited for back up to arrive or a negotiator to talk her down. Instead, you decided to pull the trigger. To take her life."

"So you think that makes us an equal?"

"Don't embarrass me. Of course we're not. I'm an artist. You. You're just a gun with a badge."

The cramp in her leg came back with a vengeance. It started as a dull flicker deep in the muscles of her leg, and then became a full-blown flex. But she couldn't stretch out. Sweat poured into her eyes. The pain was bad but the blurry vision was worse.

"Are you uncomfortable?"

The situation was unbearable she clenched her teeth and struggled with the pain in her eyes and the throbbing in her leg. She could barley she Lawson though the clouds coating her vision. It happened fast. She tried to stop it. But the pee wet her underwear and then soaked through her jeans.

"It seems you've had a little accident and that won't do."

She heard the cage door open and then felt Lawson's hand grip her wrist. He unlocked the cuffs and yanked her from the cage.

She could tell she was standing but she couldn't feel the floor beneath her feet. Pins and needles rushed through her legs. She wiped her eyes with her arm. She heard the click and then felt the cold steel of the cuff lock back around her wrist. When she opened her eyes, she realized that she was cuffed to Lawson. She took a swing at him but it was like trying to fight with a concrete block.

"Stop struggling," he said as he escorted her away from the cage and down the hall.

From this position, she could make out more of the cottage. The kitchen was off to the right. The room was large, an island with a gas range stood in the middle. The floors were ceramic, and the walls were painted dark green. They moved fast toward the back and she passed three doors, all of them closed.

He stopped suddenly, she kept her forward momentum until the steel dug into her wrist, and she was pulled back. Lawson opened the door on his right.

A bathroom.

Inside the room, Lawson moved quickly. He turned on the water and pulled the lever and water sprayed into the bathtub—it hissed from the showerhead.

"This is going to be uncomfortable but please don't try anything stupid. If you attempt another swing, I'll just stuff you back into the cage stinking of urine. Got it!"

She was just glad to be out and walking around. She wasn't stupid. She didn't see anything she could use as a weapon. There was no way she could overpower him.

I'm going to help you take off your pants. This is not something I enjoy doing, but I don't want to smell your stink, as we talk. So take a shower and clean yourself up. Clear?"

She nodded.

She unbuttoned her jeans with her left hand, and then pulled down the zipper. Lawson helped pull her pants down and she stepped out of them. Then together they slipped off her underwear.

He turned and her right hand moved with his left as he gripped her collar and tore her shirt down the middle; in one pull, like it was a wet sheet of paper. He left her bra on and told her to get into the shower.

"It's cold," she said as the water hit her skin.

He turned the knob and the water slowly increased in temperature to a comfortable level. She looked around the stall for a razor or something sharp. There was nothing but a bar of soap and a bottle of Head & Shoulders shampoo. She grabbed the bar of soap.

Their hands touched as her free hand lathered the soap over her skin.

The whole thing took less than five minutes.

They wrapped a towel around her waist before leaving the bathroom.

Out in the hallway, they turned right instead of left and she followed him like a prisoner to a room in the back.

"This is my den. See, there's the glass case I told you about."

She noticed the wood frame below the case it looked heavy and the wood shone from being polished. The case was empty. "Where's the rope?"

"Do we really need to go there?"

She shook her head.

He walked her over to a chair that sat in front of a stone fireplace and encouraged her to take a seat. She did. *Like she had a choice.*

He un-cuffed his wrist and locked the cuff around the arm of the chair.

"It's solid mahogany. I would have a tough time breaking that but go ahead, try, if you'd like.

She didn't.

The fire roared. The wood snapped and spit and the heat warmed her skin. Christine could feel the material in her bra heat up and begin to dry.

He took a seat across from her. She crossed her legs and held the towel together with her free hand.

"So what are we doing?" she asked.

"We're continuing where we left off before you had your accident."

"We know what happens to your victims so why are we prolonging the inevitable?"

"Are you in a hurry to die?"

"So that's your plan?"

"You know you're starting to irritate me. Why don't you just do yourself a favor and shut up!"

"Fine. So you killed her because she offended your assistant. I got that."

"Not because she offended Katie. Personally, I would take no offense to that, as Katie is a slut. No, it was because she thought that her breasts were too good for me to see. She had that tone that women have these days. You know what I mean?"

"No I don't."

"Like they're our equal. When I say our, I mean men. That, I wouldn't put up with. And I'll tell you she would have done anything as she hung upside down in my warehouse."

"So that's where you killed them."

"It was convenient."

"You're sick Lawson, You need help."

"Yeah my Father said that once. Do you want to know what happened to him?"

"I can guess."

"Let me tell you anyway. It's not as if I had a bad childhood. My Father was a good man. He used to take me to this same cottage when I was just a boy. He was a provider, strong, not quite as massive as me. He brought me here to teach me how to hunt. Every September, we would hunt bear. First with rifles, then, when I was older, with a crossbow. Have you ever seen an animal die in front of you? Hold its life in your hands and snuff it out at will? All the warm blood dripping from your fingers?"

His eyes were distant now, not like before, and a wave of softness washed across them as he spoke. The words chilled her and panic became an unwelcomed visitor.

"Soon, I wanted more. Animals were not enough for me. You see, that's when I decided to kill someone."

He looked at her and she tried to look away. It was as if she were frozen.

"I was nineteen and, unfortunately for my Father, he was the only one within a killings' distance. I told him first. It wasn't like I ambushed him. *He knew.* He didn't think I was serious at first but soon he must have sensed it. Hunting accident went into the police report but we know better now, don't we? So there you have it. All is out in the open. Well, I think the only true answer to *why*, is that I enjoy it. There's nothing else to it."

"That's fucked," she said and the words surprised her. They came out without any forethought, like a person suffering from Tourette syndrome.

"Oh, I think you're wrong there Detective. But that's of no importance. Your opinion that is."

He smiled, and the look scared the shit out of her.

"Please Detective, no applause, and there is no need for a standing ovation. Oh, that would be difficult for you now wouldn't it? Being handcuffed to the chair and all."

"So what happens now?"

"Do you want to live?"

She nodded. "You may not have cared about your family but I care about mine. I love them and they love me. I want to see them again. I don't want to die."

"It's simple. Kill me. That's all you have to do. That's all anyone had to do."

"Give me a gun!"

He laughed. It bounced around the room and in her ears.

"Not that easy, tomorrow. You will need to have your wits about you. You will need to hone your skills, Detective. I expect big things from you. Unlike Michael, my Father or any of the others, yes big expectations indeed. Tomorrow you will have your chance. A chance to save yourself. An opportunity to kill, or to be killed. That is your fate and so it is mine as well. The hunter and the cop. Who will win in the end? That is yet to be determined."

His words reverberated inside her. There was no doubt that he planned to kill her. She had known she was going to die ever since she woke up in the cage. Now, there was a ray of hope. A glimmer in the dark. *Indeed, a chance.*

FORTY-FIVE

Jeffries felt his wife's palm on the back of his hand. Mascara ran down her face. She looked like a female version of Alice Cooper. Her hand rubbed up and down his arm and the touch felt good. Like a fond memory. The lights in the hospital room washed everything bright white.

The sheets were tight around him and his bare ass was cold against the bed below. Sarah sat on the edge of the hospital bed. Her big blue eyes were glued to his. He could see himself in her. His nose. His eyes. The freckles that lined her cheeks—all his. Lips and cheekbones from Teresa.

Teresa stood above him, still caressing his arm. He could see by the look she gave him, that she still loved him. He would do anything for her. There was never going to be a wall between them again.

He remembered Lawson's arm around his neck. What it felt like to have a python coiled around him—the pressure. His life slowly squeezed out. The white flash of pain and the sea of darkness that followed. His last thought was of Teresa. Her smile.

Now he was alive, and Teresa was here. With him. Back again. *Christine!*

"Baby you scared me. Us," Teresa said.

"What happened to Christine?" As he asked the question, he knew from the expression on Teresa's face that something bad happened. He couldn't remember anything after he blacked out.

"You need to focus on your recovery. The police are handling it."

"Handling what. Where the fuck's Christine?"

Sarah turned away as she heard him shout, like the many times before. Teresa started crying.

"I'm sorry baby," Jefferies said. "She's my partner. I just want to know. I honestly don't remember."

"They assume that Lawson has her." She said and turned toward the window.

"Oh Shit! God help her!"

"You almost died. If they would have been five more minutes. I don't want to even think about it."

"I'm so sorry. I'm done. I'm quitting the force. As of today, I am unemployed."

Sarah looked across the bed from where she was sitting. His heart broke into a million pieces. The hurt he had caused could never be undone. He would spend the rest of his days filling her heart with happiness.

"Daddy are you going to get better?" She said.

"Honey...of course. I'll be fine. Don't you worry," he said.

Jefferies waved his daughter over. She crawled up to him and wrapped her small arms around his neck. Her breath smelled sweet, like bubble gum. She kissed him on the side of his face. His left arm shot across her back and he held her tight. Teresa returned and held his hand. He squeezed it. The tear ducts opened and warm fluid leaked out and flowed down his face.

FORTY-SIX

The chartered plane touched down at Buttonville Municipal Airport. Sandy's information was thorough. The cottage was just outside Bancroft, a small town in Northern Ontario. There was no contemplating. He had to go with his instincts and he hoped to God he was right about it...he didn't want to think about any other outcome. It had to be right. It had to be the place where Lawson took Christine.

The seatbelt sign turned off as the plane finished the taxi to the gate. He was already up and moving with his bag in his hand.

The cold air hit him without remorse. It was cold to the point of painful. He followed the yellow lines to the private entrance of Customs and Immigration. Life was easier when you had the money to fly in private charters. Inside, he approached the Customs' counter. The officer waved him over.

"Cold out there, eh?"

"That's an understatement. Listen I'm in a bit of hurry. I'm meeting some friends at a cottage."

"No problem, Mr. Hadler. I'll have you out of here in no time at all. Please place your bag on the x-ray machine."

As he placed the bag in the machine, he told the officer about the weapons inside the bag. At that point, the officer came around the counter and approached Tim.

"Please give me your license and registration for the gun and the Authorization to Transport permit."

Tim handed him the envelope containing the documents. The officer read over his travel permit. A document that Sandy forged for him before he left.

"What business are you in that you need to carry a Glock and an eight-inch hunting knife?" the officer asked.

"Is there something wrong with the documents?"

"Well, no, curious that's all."

"I'm sorry, I really am in a hurry."

The officer finished processing Tim and stamped his passport.

"Have a good day now," the officer said.

Tim left the office.

He could see the car waiting for him on the tarmac. The exhaust seeped out of the back of Cadillac CTS. It looked weighed down from the cold Canadian climate.

Thirty minutes later, he followed the direction that glowed from the GPS. The speedometer read 140km/h as he passed cars that turned into blips in the rearview mirror.

Tim traveled north on highway 404 and took the exit for Hwy 9/Newmarket. The time seemed to race by with each passing minute, and ticked away from finding Christine alive. If he could save her life, then maybe he could save his own as well.

He pulled up to an intersection and the light was red. The flashing indicator blinked on the car ahead. Each flash reminded Tim of a beating heart—Christine's heart. He turned hard on the wheel and stamped on the accelerator. He dismissed the honks coming from the cars as he ran the red light. A distant memory as the Cadillac moved north.

FORTY-SEVEN

Christine woke from a sleep she had fought hard against. She was exhausted and her body felt numb but she could move her arms. The cuffs were off. The fire died off and the room was cold. She was still wrapped in the towel from last night and her bra was dry but she was freezing. The room was quiet and there was no sign of Lawson. She rose from the chair; beside it, she noticed the pile of clothing. Her jeans were there. They looked clean. *He must have washed them.*

Christine dropped the towel and changed into her jeans. She put on a sweater that was left for her. It was too big for her and draped over her like a blanket. It was warm.

Christine walked over to the door. Opened it. She listened but heard no movement outside the room. She ran to the far end of the den to Lawson's desk and searched the drawers. She found a sharp, letter-opener and took it. The rest of the drawers contained nothing useful.

Out in the hallway, she moved like a cop, sweeping through each room with the letter-opener in her hand. She gripped it tight.

The first room she entered was the bathroom. The light was off. Moving fast, she tore open the shower curtain. Empty.

She closed the door and moved on to the next room ahead to the right.

Inside, Christine noticed the California Shutters covering the window. Thick wood shelves were built into all the walls around the room. It gave her the impression of an old library but instead of books, glass jars lined the shelves. Floating, in some sort of preservative were body parts. She winced as she saw the jar that contained breasts. She vomited when she realized that one of the jars contained something that looked like a sausage. Steam rose from the wet floor. She was appalled by her own stench. She left the room and shut the door behind her.

The final room in the hallway was smaller than the rest. About the size of her bedroom back in Manhattan. The walls were lined with rifles and shotguns hung in racks. She counted twelve. To the right, handguns floated on the wall inside a glass case.

She ran to the case and tried to slide the door open. It was locked. She moved to one of the shotguns and tried to lift it off the rack. It was held in place. Locked. All the weapons were fastened down.

Frustrated, she moved back to the glass case and slammed her elbow into it. It cracked. She hit it again and a large piece of glass fell from the top. She moved her arm just as it bounced off of the ledge and she jumped back as it shattered on the floor. She pulled the Beretta 9 mm from the wall and ejected the magazine. Empty. She pulled at the cabinet door below the case. Locked!

She jammed the letter opener where she thought the lock mechanism would be and then tried to pry the door open. After about twenty tries, and what felt like ten minutes, the lock popped. Inside, she found the 9 mm ammo she would need for the Beretta. Christine filled the magazine, and then pushed it back into the pistol grip.

When she turned, she noticed an empty space on the rack to the left. Ware marks on the wall formed the shape of crossbow. Steel arrows littered a box below. The steel shafts shone from the light and the tips looked like razor blades.

Christine left the last room.

In the hallway, she crept toward the dining room. The cage was still there but she noticed it was clean inside and she couldn't smell any trace of urine as she passed.

She looked up. The cathedral ceiling rose up forever, to places that the light dared not go. There the shadows hid all the evil her mind could conjure.

Still no a sign of Lawson.

A bag hung on the door at the entrance of the cottage. It stood out like a black house set in a field of snow.

She dumped the contents on to the solid maple table in the dining room. The loud thump of the knife made her back up. She snatched up a rolled piece of paper and untied the leather string that wrapped it.

It was a map marked with two Xs; one read you are here, the other read freedom, and between the two was a dotted line. There was a note on the bottom of the page.

Christine, by now you've probably ransacked my weapons room and equipped yourself. I knew you would! If you step out the front door with a gun in your hand, I'll pierce your heart with an arrow. Count on it! Drop the gun on the table and pick up the knife. Believe me I'll know if you haven't. Don't be stupid! Take your chances with the knife. It's the only way!

Good luck and good hunting,
Lawson

She considered the outcome and then slammed the Beretta on the table.

A puffy, white winter coat hung from a coat rack at the front entrance near the door. She pulled it off, threw it on the table beside the knife, and the map. She searched for a phone but didn't find one.

With no way of communicating with the world outside, she gathered the contents on the table minus the Glock, put on the coat, and then exited the cottage.

The snow, sucking her feet into its icy grip with each step that she took, found its way into her shoes and she shivered as it chilled her skin. She moved with stealth as she followed the marked path. She knew Lawson would be waiting but she also knew that he wouldn't lie: this was the only way out. He was close. Watching.

She moved fast and low, scanning from side to side through the rows of trees. The only sound she heard was the crunching of snow beneath her feet. The sun was high above the winter-covered landscape and its rays reflected off skeletal branches coated with ice. She wished she were wearing sunglasses because the glare from the snow interfered with her vision.

From behind, a sound echoed amongst the trees. A mere whisper. She felt the wind whip past and kiss her cheek. The steel arrow bounced off of a tree ahead of her and she ran. She wished she'd taken the gun.

Ran.

***

Two and a half hours later, Tim arrived at the cottage. He moved through the open door with the Glock in his hand. He stopped halfway in, fixated on the cage that sat in the middle of the room. The sight of it burned him. He pictured Christine inside. The cage just big enough for a large dog. How she must have felt, the fear and humiliation. Anger consumed him like nothing he had ever felt. He searched the cottage and there were no signs of her or of Lawson. She was gone. He was gone.

Outside, he found two sets of footprints in the snow. The trail flowed down the white blanket like a snake. He exhaled and his breath puffed out a fog of mist. The temperature was beyond cold: black. Noises traveled along the air. The branches of the naked trees that mixed in with the evergreens floated in the sky above. He was now moving between the trees at a good pace.

Christine's face flashed behind his eyes. Her raven hair and wide smile. The emotions she pulled out of him confused him. He liked the confusion.

The others scratched at the door to his mind, sneaking in uninvited, blending in with the image of Christine. The ones he hurt. He shook his head and scattered the ghosts to the dark crevasses of his mind.

Focus.

He found the arrow.

***

She looked back beyond the branches of the evergreens. The hard pine needles scraped at the skin on her face as she hid behind the tree and used its branches for cover. She could see him as he walked down the trail toward her. The black crossbow in his left hand contrasted against the white snowsuit he wore.

She moved back behind the line of evergreens. The angle blocked her view of Lawson, which meant that he wouldn't be able to see her either. She took the only chance she had. She bolted. The snow beneath her was softer as she ran the line she picked out. Her legs burned and she was thirsty, but she pumped away.

"Detective. Detective. Detective," Lawson called out from somewhere behind her. She felt a pinch in her thigh.

She fell to the right and the soft powder welcomed her with cold arms. The warm throb in her leg felt wet. She reached back and touched the cold steel of the arrow. Her arm shook as the tips of her fingers tapped on the shaft. She grunted out from the pain.

"Now that's sad, Detective. That was way too easy. Oh, this won't do. No, this won't do at all," Lawson said.

She turned to face him with the knife in her hand hidden under the snow. He towered over her. The sun was high above him and the rays reflected off of the steel arrow in the chamber.

"You're no hunter, Lawson." She said.

Her breath left her with a suddenness that caused panic. She felt her eyes bulge from their sockets and she peed as his boot pulled away from her stomach. She tried to scream out but had no breath to do so.

"Sorry, Detective. I didn't hear you correctly. Please repeat that."

She said nothing; instead, curled up and waited.

He crouched down close enough that she could feel the warmth of his breath against her mouth.

"That's what I thought. You had every opportunity to fight. Instead you ran. Ran like a scared little animal. Like a rabbit. Now look at you. Pathetic."

The snow fell away as she moved her hand from the cold white blanket. Lawson's eyes widened as they shot from Christine's eyes to the hand that was now at his side. At her hand that was gripping the knife that was now inside him. He looked back at her with a level of shock that she was sure surprised even him.

He pushed her hand aside and the knife came away with it, blood dripping from the steel, staining the snow below it. He stood up. The look on his face turned from shock to anger. He aimed the crossbow at Christine's face. Their eyes met and she was ready. At least she had tried. At least, she had hurt him. She thought about her family and, for some strange reason, about Tim. *She would miss them. She didn't want to die. God, she didn't want to die.*

"Lawson!"

A voice shouted out in the cold. Christine thought she was dreaming but Lawson turned and she knew she wasn't. The blood wet her face in small splashes. It was warm. She opened her eyes to see Lawson's shoulder pouring blood. The crossbow dropped from his hand and buried itself in the snow with its grip sticking up.

***

Tim heard the voice coming from behind the evergreens. It was Lawson and he was close. He moved faster, past the row of trees. His eyes flashed from Lawson to Christine. She was hard to make out, almost hidden by the size of him. She was there—and she was alive.

"Lawson!"

Tim aimed the gun at Lawson, pulled the trigger, as Lawson turned around to face him. The white coat exploded from the back and small feathers soaked with blood fell to the snow below. Lawson dropped what looked like a gun as Tim approached.

The two killers met eye to eye. *Was he sulking?*

"Move, and I'll put a bullet in your mouth!" Tim said.

"Tim?" Christine said.

Tim motioned for Lawson to move toward a birch tree and away from Christine. He did. Lawson's back hit against the tree and he almost slipped past.

"Ok, wait a minute. Just wait a minute," Lawson said.

Tim pulled the trigger and Lawson's snowsuit opened up where his kneecap should be.

"Tim!" Christine said.

He could see Lawson shift his weight to his other leg and Tim squeezed the trigger again. Lawson fell to his knees and screamed out. The tree held him upright as the blood soaked the snow below him.

"Tim! Wait!" Christine said

Tim ignored her and jammed the gun into his pocket. He pulled out the large Bowie. The blade gleamed in the sunshine. He turned the knife before Lawson's face.

"Lawson, I have to say I'm not impressed. I would think that someone like you would have been smarter than this. Look at you. You call Christine pathetic." Tim slid the blade across Lawson's face, opening the skin, revealing the cheekbone underneath.

"Tim! Stop! Tim, please stop!" she said.

Lawson made a failed attempt to grab the knife from Tim's hand. His arm flopped away as Tim pushed it aside. He met Lawson's eyes as the blade's tip moved through the material of Lawson's coat, passed the liner, and into flesh. Lawson growled as the blade slipped all the way in.

"Tim, wait! Please wait! That's enough!" Christine said.

He heard her shouting and tuned her out, as he forced the knife downward in a carving motion. Blood soaked the coat and stained it red. Lawson collapsed toward him.

"Oh my God, Tim, what did you do?"

"What had to be done," he said.

He turned from the lifeless body and rushed to Christine who was now standing. He held her in his arms. Her tears wet his cheek and as his face met hers. Her arms were over his but not hugging back.

"Tim, I don't understand. How did you..."

"Please, Christine, don't worry about anything. I'm here now. You're safe and that's all I care about. You're all I care about."

She backed away a few inches and stared at him for a moment. He could tell she was struggling with something. He realized what had just happened and what it must have looked like to her. At that moment, a ball of steel dropped in his stomach and it knotted up. His back muscles tensed and a thousand neurons fired all at once.

Christine's eyes closed and she wrapped her arms around him and kissed his mouth.

"You're right. I don't care. Tim, thank you for coming for me."

The release was instantaneous and the pressure he felt only seconds ago evaporated into the winter air.

FORTY-EIGHT

Two weeks later in Manhattan, Jeffries hugged Christine. The two held each other to the point where others around them would feel uncomfortable from the embrace. Other officers moved around them.

Jefferies pulled away.

"I don't understand. How did you do it? Christine, the guy was a maniac," Jeffries said.

"It took everything I had in me. I almost died up there. I don't remember much before the confrontation. Just that I ended up being the one alive in the end," she said.

"Well, we're all happy for that. You know the RCMP sent a report down. It looks like they still haven't found a body yet and they won't be able to do a full search until the spring. They said that it's possible that Lawson might end up being food for the wild."

"Honestly, I really don't want to talk about this anymore. You know what I mean?"

"Hey, no problem."

"So tell me, how are you going to like working behind a desk?" she asked.

"I'm looking forward to it. Teresa moved back."

"That's good. That's really good," she said.

"What about you? When do start back?"

Christine moved around to her desk and pulled out her chair.

"Right now."

"Well, it's great to have you back Christine," Jefferies squeezed her shoulder as he moved past. She was alone at her desk and her thoughts.

She did what she had to do all right: whatever she had to, to save Tim. Something changed inside her that day up in Canada. She lost a part of herself. The part that drove her to become a cop. The guiding edge between right and wrong. He loved her and she loved him. He saved her and at that moment, Tim became a killer. She couldn't look at him the same after that but she couldn't judge him either. If it weren't for him, she wouldn't be alive to cast judgment.

She reached into her purse and placed the picture frame on her desk. The picture was of Tim and her, and in the background the sun was setting on the Jamaican sky.

They were both smiling.

EPILOGUE

The plane touched down in Austin-Bergstrom International Airport and then taxied to the terminal.

Tim pulled his leather carry-on from the over-head compartment, and strolled up to the exit. The cabin was smaller than most he was accustomed to; he had to duck his head to avoid hitting the roof. The springy blonde thanked him for flying with the airline and smiled as she said good-bye.

Outside in the rental car, Tim punched Rebecca's address into the GPS and then pulled out of the parking garage. The moon was smeared red. It floated in the middle of dark Texas sky. The blackness behind the stars was void of light it was as if the moon and the stars were inside the earth's atmosphere. He felt rejuvenated, exonerated, and like his old self. He thought about Christine. He wasn't sure what was going to happen with her or if they would ever have a resolution to their problem but those were thoughts for later days. Right now he had only Rebecca on his mind. Retribution!

    She would realize that in this world, in his world, Newton's third law governed: *"Every action has an equal and opposite reaction"*. She was in for a world of pain.

ABOUT THE AUTHOR

Dwayne Kavanagh, as a child, found comfort in the dark corners of his imagination. In 2005, he sat down in a small home office and let the stories transfer from those lightless caverns to the bright screen of his laptop computer and has been scribbling every day since.

Dwayne was born in Toronto and raised in Burlington, Ontario, Canada. He lives with his Fiancée, Nicky and her sports fanatic son Lucas, and with unconditional love for his beautiful daughters Megan and Emily, in southern Ontario.